REASON TO LOVE

SEDONA VENEZ

WANT FREE SEDONA VENEZ BOOKS?

Sign up for Sedona Venez's Newsletter and receive FREE BOOKS. In addition to the free stories, you will also get special pricing, exclusive previews and news of new releases.

GET A FREE SEDONA VENEZ BOOK!

Join Sedona's mailing list to be the first to know of new releases, free books, special prices and other author giveaways.

https://sedonavenez.com/free-book

❧ I ❧

REASON

SITTING behind my desk in the corner office on the tenth floor of my Midtown Manhattan building, I listened to two vampire brothers—both middle-aged, well dressed, and pompous as all hell—explaining their legal woes before me. Each held an envelope torn at the top, sheaths for documents critical to their current dispute with their vampire ex-fiancée.

Clasping my fingers together, I eyed the animated brothers. Just another typical day at the Orlov firm with entitled pure-blooded vampires wanting to file silly, ridiculous cases against each other.

As an attorney for wealthy Other shifters, vampires, and assorted supernatural beings—clients, I thought I'd heard and seen it all until the brothers started to spell out their wish to sue for their ex's embryos.

I blinked and then blinked again.

Wait, what? The ones that come from within their ex's body?

I reclined and bounced slowly in my chair, my eyes following each brother in turn as he spoke. So far, I'd done business in five languages today—Russian, Mandarin, German, Italian, and English. My assistant, Tabitha, had yet to bring me my dinner, a meal of Moroccan chicken with couscous, vegetables, and pick-

I

les. Somewhat distracted by thoughts of food, I tried to concentrate on the Italian conversation going on in front of me, occasionally punctuated with English for technical terms like *deposition* and *contractual agreement.*

Jesus, why are they fucking my day up with this bullshit?

My eyes flicked down when my cell buzzed, and Storm's number appeared on the screen. One brother frowned, disapprovingly staring at my cell and then at me, the loose skin under his neck making him look like a Shar-Pei. Sighing, I let the call roll to voice mail.

"Have you heard a thing we said, young lady?" the second brother, who had a weird handlebar mustache, asked me in Italian.

In the same language, I counted argumentative points off on my fingers, delving into the finer nuances of the argument without losing focus, and returned to the central point in a similar way a quiet pack of wolves would encircle a deer.

"I'll do what I can to help," I finished in English.

The two brothers watched uncomfortably.

Shar-Pei Neck shook his head, causing the skin to jiggle like Jell-O. "No. We want your father to handle this." His cheeks became flushed.

"Would you mind clarifying why?" I asked.

"We don't want you as our attorney because you're a... a—" stuttered Shar-Pei.

Shit, here we go again.

"Hybrid vampire." I cut him off while coolly assessing them. "Be that as it may, my father has his hands full with Orlov coven business. So, gentlemen, it's me or nothing." My lips pursed with displeasure while I drummed my well-manicured nails against my mahogany desk.

Pure-blooded vampires, like these brothers, were elitist asswipes, and I hated dealing with them. If it were up to me, I'd flip them the bird before kicking them the hell out of my office. But I had no authority to do so. Dad called the shots. This was his firm, and I was just a well-paid attorney on his payroll.

I resented the fact that Dad's pure-blooded vampire clients refused to view hybrids like me as anything but an abomination, weak and beneath them. Essentially, from their perspective, I was incapable of handling their legal affairs.

Granted, Dad had built the Orlov firm by managing the legal affairs of highbrow Others for years, but frankly, it was time for a change. And for over a year, I'd been staging a one-woman campaign in hopes of finally being made partner, so I would have the power to transform the firm and the types of clients we represented. But so far, it'd been to no avail. As far as Dad was concerned, his clients weren't the problem; I was.

"How old are you, beautiful?" Handlebar Mustache sneered with his eyes focused on my ample breasts.

I snapped my fingers. "Hey! Up here."

He leered in an icky way that said he didn't give a shit.

I blew out my cheeks. *Sexist fucking vampires.*

I couldn't care less that I didn't necessarily fit into the comfortable stereotypes of how a female vampire looked or how a successful woman dressed. Most vampires were beautiful and lithe, while my features were more exotic—or what guys might call sensual. I could live with that description. My body was tight and curvy, and I had more ass and breasts than should be allowed on any woman—unless her lifelong ambition was to be a very well-paid stripper.

This was me, a hybrid vampire—vampire father, human mother—and I didn't want to change a damn thing. And I refused to let Dad's clients diminish my accomplishments and hard work.

"First, my name is Reason Orlov, not *beautiful*. Second, it's never polite to ask a woman's age."

I didn't bother to point out that, at only eighteen years old—five years ago—I was the youngest person ever sworn in and admitted to the New York State Bar, making me the youngest attorney at that time. Now, at twenty-three, I'd paid my dues after coming to work for Dad, a legendary New York attorney, who was also an ornery SOB most of the time.

I'd proven my worth by busting my ass and bringing in younger, wealthier new clients who tripled the Orlov firm's revenue within four months of me being hired. I'd also smiled and swallowed the hurt like a bitter pill when Dad refused to make me an equal partner in the firm until his pure-blooded clients "got more comfortable" with me.

But I was a realist. I had human blood running through my veins, so I knew they would never hire me as their attorney.

Shar-Pei puffed out his cheeks. "Listen, young lady, we don't give a shit what you think. If we don't hear from your father within twenty-four hours, we're taking our business elsewhere."

Good riddance.

"I'm sorry to hear that," I answered while pushing back from my desk. "We've really appreciated your business over the years."

I moved around the desk. The brothers stood up while eyeballing me.

"But sometimes, change is good for all parties involved." I ushered them toward my office door.

"You'd best believe we'll be calling your father, young lady." Handlebar threatened.

"You do that." I smiled. "Have a great day, gentlemen," I chirped.

Returning to my desk, I tiredly flopped down onto my plush leather seat. "Damn, the drama never stops here," I mumbled, going back to my laptop and searching for information on the next client.

Tabitha rushed in with my dinner. "Jesus, the idiot brothers looked absolutely livid." She cleared a space on my desk and laid out my dinner with a bottle of Pellegrino. "Another client bites the dust, huh?"

"Fortunately," I quipped. "I'm polite and straightforward, but they refuse to comprehend that I won't put up with their patronizing shit. Between the clients and my dad, every damn day, it's a battle just to do my fucking job." Starving, I dug into my dinner. "Maybe it's time for me to wave the white flag and just quit."

The writing was on the wall; Dad was never going to make me partner, and his clients would never accept me for who and what I was.

"I agree. Maybe you should quit," Tabitha replied. "Working here has changed you, and not for the better. Where's the I-want-to-make-a-difference woman I've known for years?"

"Gone," I countered.

But she was right. I wasn't happy at work. And I damn sure wasn't happy in my personal life. But to give it all up—my six-figure income, my lavish lifestyle, and the prestige of working for the Orlov firm—would leave a bitter taste in my mouth.

"Frankly, the thought of starting over with nothing scares the shit out of me." I swallowed hard. "Besides, there's no way in hell I'm going to give Dad's snobby clients the satisfaction of thinking they finally ran me out of the firm with my tail tucked between my legs."

Tabitha shook her head with a disapproving glare. "The crazy things we tell ourselves to justify our inability to take a risk and push the edges of our comfort zone."

"Oh, shut up," I grumbled even though she'd hit the nail right on the head. "What does the rest of my schedule look like?"

"Three more appointments, and you're done for the day."

I frowned. "That's it?"

"It's a short day because you have that Orlov formal event thing tonight."

My fork stopped midway to my mouth. "Oh God"—I swallowed—"that's tonight?" *Shit, I completely forgot about it.*

Tabitha nodded. "Don't worry. I picked up your couture gown from the designer and dropped it off at your place. So after your last appointment, you'll have plenty of time to get home, take a long, hot bath, and properly pamper yourself."

I scrunched my nose with distaste just thinking about the

purpose of tonight's event and the guests attending for another opportunity to kiss Dad's ass. But it was my duty to attend these high-profile events as the daughter of *the* Oskar Orlov, the Vampire King—the most powerful vampire, not only in NYC, but also in the Northeast.

Or I could just skip the soiree altogether. But I knew Dad would serve my head on a platter, rotisserie-style, if I shunned his precious Blood Rite ceremony. Over the course of the month, I had made several adamant pleas for him to cancel the atrocious event, but to no avail. Dad was steadfast in his belief that, with the Shadows slithering around Manhattan, trying to promote a war between the Others, tonight's Blood Rite was more important than ever, and the Orlov coven must present a united front.

His united-front point I couldn't debate. The coven was already whirling about the fact that Dad's former second-in-command, Dimitri, had allegedly been killed by shifters. Now rumors were circulating that Dad was next on the shifters' hit list. Vampires were like sharks, and when they smelled blood in the water, they would begin circulating, waiting for Dad's impending death. If Dad died, vampires waiting in the dark, plotting on taking over his throne of power, wouldn't hesitate to kill me, the last of the Orlovs and next in line for the throne.

Tabitha tilted her head to the side. "So are you finally going to tell me what the Orlov celebration is for?"

"I would, but then I'd have to kill you," I deadpanned.

Tabitha gulped with wide eyes.

"Jesus. I'm kidding, Tabitha. But really... I can't tell you. Believe me, you're better off not knowing."

"Got it. Okay, I'll leave you to your dinner." She started to waltz out and then stopped. "Oh, and Stefan called five times today. When are you two supposed to get married?"

"Never," I snapped.

Every time I thought about Dad's favorite kiss-ass enforcer,

Stefan, I could feel an anxious knot tightening in my throat, making me feel like I was suffocating.

Tabitha arched a brow. "But didn't your father preordain that you two get hitched and pop out a shitload of vampire babies?"

I shuddered at the truth of her words. Time was running out. Soon, there would be no more dodging this bullet. My marriage to Stefan was imminent. Bile rushed up my throat at the thought. Stefan and I had practically grown up with each other. He would follow me around, trying to run my life, and I would deliberately taunt him. It didn't help that Dad had taken a liking to him, grooming him for years to become his head enforcer—a position recently vacated due to the death of Dimitri. Now Stefan was drunk with power and pushing for us to get married.

"Stefan is wasting his time. I would never be interested in a man like him."

Stefan's arrogance was one of the many things that turned me off about him. Well, that and the fact that he was coldhearted and calculating, and he would do anything to get ahead. A chill zipped down my spine when I thought about the number of humans and Others Stefan had murdered to prove his loyalty as one of Dad's most trusted enforcers.

There was also the most important fact; Stefan viewed me as another rung to get him closer to power. Unfortunately, he was the son Dad never had but wanted. Stefan had slayed his way and smoothly slid into the coveted position as Dad's head enforcer and second-in-command. But his career ambitions went way beyond that. He wanted power to rule the Orlov coven. And I was his ticket to greatness as the only heir.

"I bet your father would be pissed if he knew that."

I scowled, remembering the last argument I'd had with Dad about this very topic. Rocking back in my chair, I eyed Tabitha. "I've told him I won't marry Stefan. But he's so obsessed with marrying his hybrid-vampire daughter off that he's chosen to take another route to get me to alter my decision—pushing Stefan toward me for every social event he can muster."

I pursed my lips. "I just don't understand why Others think being a single woman is a fate worse than death. I don't need a man. Shit, I think it's dangerous to need anyone." I'd learned that hard lesson years ago. "And if I chose to take him as my mate, it'd be because the survival of the Orlov coven depended on it."

My heart and soul would never be his. If I took him as my consort, it would be a business arrangement, not for love. Not that Stefan would give a shit. Love was a foreign concept to vampires. Unfortunately, as a hybrid vampire—part human and vampire—the concept of affection and love was not lost on me. I craved it, but my destiny had already been written in stone.

Love is not part of my life equation.

"Hell, you're preaching to the choir. No matter how hard I try, I still can't make my mother understand why my sole ambition in life is not finding a rabbit-shifter mate and popping out a shitload of rabbit-shifter babies." Tabitha sighed heavily. "And when I told her I was dating a bear-shifter, she nearly had a stroke."

"Overbearing parents," I mumbled.

"Hear, hear, my friend," Tabitha replied before leaving my office.

I stared down at my barely touched meal, pushing it aside. I'd lost my appetite. My eyes flicked over to the corner of my desk at the framed photo of Light, Storm, Sky, Demi, and me hanging out on the sunny, white sandy beach, drunk as hell and making a lot of alcohol-induced bad decisions.

Shit, I missed the old days when we had been carefree with no responsibilities.

I sighed heavily. Now, between our busy lives and careers, we could barely find time for each other. It didn't help that, in the span of a couple weeks, Light and Storm—cousins and business partners—had found their mates. Storm was with Knox Gunner, a badass rock star and wolf-shifter, and Light was with Ryker Alfero, alpha of one of the largest and most powerful wolf-shifter packs in New York, leader of the Other Council, and Knox's brother. I was happy as hell my besties had finally found love, but damn, I missed them something fierce.

My cell rang. Quickly swiping it, I answered, "Hey, Storm. I was just—"

"Reason," Storm cut in, "she's gone." She sobbed as if her heart were breaking.

I leaped to my feet with heart-racing fear. I'd never heard her cry like this. "Who's gone?"

I received no response. Storm was still wailing, clearly hysterical. Panic clogged my throat.

No. Calm down, Reason. Take control of this situation.

"Storm, listen to me," I ordered. "Let me speak to Knox."

I paced back and forth, waiting impatiently.

I heard Storm's footsteps and then Knox yelling in the background, as if talking to someone else.

"Hold on, Ryker," Knox stated loudly. "Storm," he crooned, "I thought you were going to lie down. Baby, I need you to relax. I told you we're handling it."

"Stop treating—oh, just forget it." Storm hiccupped. "Here. Reason."

"Reason?" he asked into Storm's phone.

Wasting no time, I demanded, "Knox, what the fuck is going on?"

"Light's been kidnapped."

My legs wobbled. "The Shadows," I whispered. It was a statement, not a question.

This wasn't the Shadows'—a clan of fanatic warlocks obsessed with breeding with the Credence family to create a new race of fae—first attempt at kidnapping Light. A couple nights ago, Light's grandfather had sent his two minions to Redemption —a well-known upscale, private restaurant notorious for its anything-goes vibe, owned by Vivica, a vampire and close friend of Dad's—to nab Light. The plan had been foiled by her estranged father and her mate Ryker, along with his pack.

According to the Credence family, the Shadows had done some crazy things to show their devotion to the fae, even offering their wives to them in hopes the fae would breed with them. But thank goodness, the fae had refused. Shit had gone to hell when the fae disappeared off this planet. That was when the Shadows had started stalking the Credences, a family of fae-witch hybrids.

"How?" I croaked. My heart fluttered like a trapped bird.

"Reason, I can't get into the details right now. I'm on my cell with Ryker. If you want details, head over to Ryker's headquarters where the pack is mobilizing. I'll text you the address."

Our call ended, and I just stood there with my mind whirling, frantically searching for how I could help. Then one name popped into my head. The only man I knew with enough power, connections, and resources to help Ryker.

Placing my cell on speaker, I voice-dialed him.

"Dad, listen, the Shadows have—"

"I know," he replied sharply.

My eyes narrowed. "You know what?"

"The Shadows have Light."

My entire body went cold. "And you didn't think to pick up the phone and tell me?"

"It has nothing to do with my coven."

"Come again?" I slumped against the edge of the desk, chest and limbs feeling tight.

"It's not personal. Just business."

I jumped to my feet, pacing back and forth, screaming into the cell, "Light is like my sister. She's family. Not to mention the fact that we've been the Credence family's attorney for centuries."

"I only protect what's mine. You and the Orlov coven."

I stared into space, dumbfounded. "But the Shadows are everyone's problem now since they've figured out how to harvest Other organs. Their next step will be selling the organs on the black market to humans. Then the Shadows will start hunting Others like animals just to keep up with demand."

"As I said before, you and the Orlov coven."

"I can't do this, Dad." I swiped my cell, ending the call.

Grabbing my handbag, I raced out of the office. The Shadows were crazy and would stop at nothing to get what they wanted. If Light had to die, she would be just another casualty in their war against the Others. And I was scared to fucking death of a world without Light in it.

Tabitha sputtered, "Where are you going? You have three more clients to see."

"Cancel my appointments. My family needs me."

I SIGHED WITH RELIEF WHEN THE TAXI PULLED UP TO RYKER'S headquarters. Wasting no time, I paid and hopped out before running into the building's nearly deserted lobby, except for the dark-haired man leaning against the security desk. With muscles bunching against his crisp white tailored shirt, it was hard not to notice the wolf-shifter staring at me.

Damn. What's Jackal doing here?

Tilting my head, I boldly glared at him. He was hot—well, hot and scary. He didn't even smile. In fact, he was scowling at me, menace pouring from him like a dark cloud. His searing eyes made me want to fidget. His stark features blended well with his chiseled cheekbones and painfully hard jaw, and his body was pure rippling muscle. But Jackal was completely not my type. I wasn't interested in shifters. And I was damn sure I wasn't remotely close to his type of woman, which included being a wolf-shifter, submissive, blond, and petite.

He arched his eyebrow at me. When he crossed his corded, muscular arms, my eyes traveled up his tall, well-built body, stopping at his piercing bright-green eyes. Inexplicably, my fingers clenched, fighting the need to run through his blunt-cut, midnight-black hair.

Shit, shit, shit. Bad hybrid.

Forcing a slow gait rather than rushing toward him, I stopped in front of him. Tossing my hair in loose waves over my shoulder, I licked my full bottom lip. Awareness strummed through me. Firmly planting my feet, I gathered my strength until the menace shrouding him like a veil ceased to intimidate me.

I forced my gaze to linger on him. "What did I do to deserve my very own welcoming wolf-shifter?"

His eyes traveled from the top of my head down my curvy body, encased in a pin-striped, double-breasted blazer and matching miniskirt. I refused to let him ruffle my feathers like he always seemed to do. This was attorney Reason. Hyper-composed Reason. Fashionable, elegant, in-charge Reason.

"Knox asked me to brief you on the Light situation," he said evenly.

"How bad is it?" I croaked.

"A shitstorm," he grunted. "In a nutshell, all hell broke out this morning when Ryker, Light, Rip, Soar, and I were heading over to Ava and Lia's house to discuss a lead they'd found on their missing client list." He ran a hand over his head. "And, bam, a car came out of fucking nowhere, slamming into Ryker and Light. He got trapped behind the wheel, but Light managed to get out of the car. Rip, Soar, and I couldn't get to her in time. We were pinned down by gunfire." He scowled. "The Shadows seized the opportunity and snatched Light." He made a sweeping arm gesture. "We were supposed to protect Light, our alpha female, and we fucking failed." His nostrils flared with anger, the look in his eyes bleak, haunted.

I reached out a hand to comfort him and then sharply pulled it back. "Jackal, you're beating yourself up for something you couldn't control."

"I'm the pack's enforcer and the second-highest-ranking member. It was my job to protect her. This is my fuckup." He cracked his knuckles. "And I won't rest until we find out where that fucker Baptiste Thomas is holding Light."

"Baptiste Thomas?"

"Leader of the Shadows and Light's grandfather."

I rubbed my forehead, feeling the onset of a migraine. "So what's his endgame?"

"He wants to use Light to create a new race of fae," he growled.

"Jesus." Bile rushed up my throat. "We've got to get her back and fast."

"We're working on it," Jackal gritted out.

"I asked my father to help with resources and contacts to find Light," I blurted, feeling like shit that Dad had said no. "But he refused. I'm sorry." Tears pricked my eyes, but I held them back like a dam.

His eyes narrowed. "Did you honestly think he would?"

"I feel like an idiot, but yes, I did. Everything is not lost. I'll keep nagging him until he does. I swear."

He shook his head. "That shit is not going to happen, darling."

The sad thing was Jackal was right. Dad wouldn't budge from his position unless there was something in it for him.

And then it dawned on me that I had one more card to play with Dad. Tonight, I would have to make a deal with the devil. A deal that would cause all types of trouble. It was not my first choice, but to earn his help with getting Light back, I would do anything.

Glancing down at my watch, there was still enough time for me to get home and get ready for the Blood Rite. "I've got to go. Knox has my number, so tell him to give me a call if you have any updates on Light."

I turned on my heels, heading out the door. I started to hail a cab when I heard Jackal's husky voice directly behind me.

"Reason, I'll drive you home. It's not safe out here with those crazy Shadows running around."

I frowned. "I'm safe, Jackal. Everyone knows not to fuck with me. My father is notoriously insane."

"But you'll be safer with me."

I shrugged, too mentally and emotionally exhausted to argue with him. Plus, I didn't relish in being alone right now. "All right, let's go."

~

THERE WAS A COMFORTABLE SILENCE AS JACKAL RACED through Manhattan.

"How's Ryker doing?" I asked.

"Not great," he snapped. "He's losing his mind. It's never good when a newly mated shifter is separated from his mate. Believe me." He scowled with a vein pulsing along his jawline.

The air was suddenly thick with tension, and frankly, I didn't know what I'd said to piss him off.

Clearing my throat, I asked, "Has security been beefed up for Ava and Lia?"

From experience, I knew Storm's mother Ava and Light's mother Lia were not easily rattled and had a wealth of connections that would come in handy with helping find Light. But they were still in danger. The whole Credence bloodline was.

"They're fine. They called in a few favors to get extra security." His cell rang. "Hold on, Reason. I need to take this." He tapped his earpiece. "What's up, Rip?" He paused. "That's not good. Okay, I'll go pay him a visit. Lean on him a little and make him give up intel. No. I'm driving Reason home." He paused. "Oh, shut the hell up. I'll check in with you later. And keep an eye on Ryker. He's coming apart at the seams. Later."

It dawned on me that I knew very little about the members of Ryker's pack, including Jackal.

"So how did all you guys meet each other?" I asked.

Jackal shrugged. "Soar, Rip, and I met in the military. We worked on some secret missions together. And we met Ryker when he saved Rip's life." He rubbed his head. "Rip's heart had fucking stopped after he was injured during our last mission.

Hell, we'd thought he was a goner. That's why we nicknamed him Rip—Restin Peace. When we got to the hospital, Ryker was the cardiologist on call, and he brought Rip back to life. We've been friends ever since.

"So it wasn't much of a decision when Ryker asked us to come back to New York with him to rebuild his pack. He's our leader. We respect and trust him with our lives, and we would do anything to help him get his mate back. Light's our alpha female, and she has earned a spot in each of our hearts."

I blinked back the tears. Damn, these shifters were a fucking fierce, awesome family. When I thought about the coldness of the members of my coven, there was just no comparison.

"So how did you and Light become friends?" he asked. "A fae witch and vampire aren't usually friends; the two races don't have much in common."

I bit my lower lip, debating on just how much I wanted him to know about me or my friendships with Light and Storm beyond my often-standard response that we'd met through my family since I was a part of a long line of attorneys who had handled all their family's legal affairs for centuries. Not many cared that our relationship had been cemented because Others ostracized us for being different. It was hell being hybrids. The Other kids hadn't exactly lined up to be our friends. We weren't Other enough to fit into their world and too Other to blend into the human world.

"Technically, I'm a hybrid vampire. My mother is human, and you know what my dad is. Frankly, Light and I have everything in common. We're hybrids." I eyed him. "Others kill and hunt us for sport. Light, Storm, and I are hated by Others because, in their eyes, we are abominations."

He snorted. "Others have always been afraid of anything different. Hybrids aren't the threat. Vampires are."

I stiffened. "Excuse me?"

"You heard me. Vampires don't abide by rules. They kill indiscriminately. I can't tell you how many missions I was assigned back in the day to take out some rogue vampire horde making trouble by killing or turning humans."

I glared at him. "That's an ignorant thing to say, shifter. Vampires have rules. It's called the vampire covenant, and if a vampire breaks it, they are severely punished by their coven's vampire king or queen. The rogues you hunted did not belong to a coven and were a blight —not only to humans, but also to all good vampires."

"Good vampires?" He laughed. "There's no such thing, darling."

I rolled my eyes. "I'm not about to waste my energy on why what you just said is total bullshit. But I hear you loud and clear, shifter. You don't like vampires." It was a statement, not a question.

"No," he hissed.

The animosity between shifters and vampires wasn't new; it was deeply rooted in centuries-old rivalry. But for some reason, his obvious dislike of my kind pissed me off more than it should have.

"Message received, asshole," I bit out, relieved we were finally approaching my tree-lined townhouse only a few steps from Central Park. "Pull over to the left." I jabbed my finger in the direction. "My townhouse is the one in the middle."

He double-parked and turned off his vehicle. Hopping out, he walked around the automobile, opening my door. As soon as my feet hit the ground, I tried not to flinch when he put his hand on the small of my back, guiding me toward my townhouse, then up the stairs.

Digging into my handbag, I located my keys before we reached my front door. Not even bothering to turn around to face him, I casually declared, "So you can get my number from Knox. Give me a call if you have any updates on Light. Day or night, just call." Turning the key and unlocking the door, I was desperate to put an end to my time with Jackal.

"Is that the only reason you would want me to call you?"

My fingers stilled before I turned robotically to face him. There was an eerily familiar predatory gleam in his eyes. It was the same marauding stare I would give men I was determined to sample in order to scratch my sexual itch. But that was before I'd changed my simpering vixen ways.

My life of looking for love and sex in all the wrong places was done. I wanted more in a man and a relationship, and Jackal for damn sure wasn't it.

His lips curled up into a sensual smile with beautiful whites on display. I bit back the hysterical bubble of laughter at the cocky, sexy smile that I was positive had countless women—Others and humans alike—melting at his feet.

"Why else?" I replied.

His smile disappeared.

My eyes widened with fake dismay. "Oh... I see. You actually thought I was interested in being a member of your freaky sex circus." I patted him on the head like a puppy. "Sorry. Not interested."

His canines lengthened to menacing points.

I bit back a snicker before saying, "Why are you mad? Just suck it up, buttercup."

With beefy arms crossed and eyes disapprovingly staring at me, he replied, "Let's get one thing clear, vampire. I'm not interested in sleeping with you. All I'm saying is I'm here for you if you need anything."

I snorted. *Uh-huh.*

I cocked my head. "Okay, I'm going to break it down for you like you're a two-year-old because I have places to be tonight. I'm not interested in being your next fuck toy. Besides, you and I know I'm not your type."

"Type?" he growled.

"A woman who's not afraid to knock your cocky ass down a couple notches. Good night, shifter."

Quickly turning around and placing my hand on the doorknob, I yelped when I felt his saucer-sized palms plop down on my shoulders before turning me around to face him.

"What the hell are you doing?" I squeaked.

He released his grip and grabbed my waist, roughly pulling me forward. "Are you scared, vampire?" His eyebrow lifted.

I refused to move away from him. I didn't back away from anything. Never had; never would. "Of what?"

My unease heightened when he watched me with that delicious intensity, which immediately made me all hot and jittery.

"This," he grunted.

He arched down, grabbing my face between his callused palms, and a weird jolt of energy pulsed through me. Instead of pushing him away, strangely, the only thing I could think of was how long it'd been since I felt a man's hands on my skin. His full focus was on me, the attention sending little tremors of awareness through me, as we stared at each other, speechless, our faces mere inches apart.

Move, Reason. Just fucking go.

My mind and body staged a mutiny by refusing to cooperate, as if daring the shifter to make another move. He did by pressing his lips against mine.

No, no, no. This will not do.

Reaching up, I slapped my hands against his wide shoulders with every intention of shoving him away. Instead, my fingers gripped him tight, pulling him closer. My lips parted before he sucked my tongue into his mouth.

Oh, Baby Jesus. Why does he taste like my three favorite things— coffee, mint, and cinnamon?

My tongue slid around the tip of his and then rubbed under it. My body throbbed with need, and every cell was focused on him. His hand slid up to my neck, possessively grabbing the back of my head, while the other shifted to my ass, lightly touching, before he softly kissed my throat. The contradiction between the hardness of his grip on my hair and the gentleness of his kiss sent a shiver down my spine while my mind imagined all the other fun, naughty things his mouth could do.

How would his tongue feel against my cunt? Would he flick it fast? Slow? Suck it? Nibble it?

Damn, the freaky and sensual possibilities were fucking endless.

Lost in my lust-induced reverie, I moaned from the loss of his lips when he abruptly stepped back, breaking off our kiss.

"So you're not interested, huh?" He winked at me. "By the way, do you know you purr when you get all hot and bothered?"

"You fucking—" I sputtered.

"I'll be seeing you around, vampire." He turned on his heel and jogged down the stairs while whistling happily.

I opened my door with jerky movements before crossing the threshold and slamming the door behind me. As I stood in the darkened foyer, my hands clenched with rage at how easily Jackal had strummed me like a guitar.

"Okay, you won that round, you cunt-teasing evil bastard," I hissed, tightening my fists in anger. "But next round, get ready for cracked nuts and a world of pain, shifter."

❦ 2 ❦

JACKAL

"Fuck," I hissed while running my hands through my sweat-dampened hair. "This shit is not happening."

Every damn time I shut my eyes, the vision of Reason Orlov strutting into the headquarters lobby with her fierce confidence and wickedly luscious body would taunt me. Calling me to fuck her in every freaky, dirty position I could imagine. Even after I convinced myself that my fixation with the vampire was fleeting.

Sleep had been elusive for hours when, mercifully, I'd finally drifted to oblivion. Only to be plagued by a dream of taking the hybrid vampire from behind while clutching a fistful of her thick auburn hair as I rode her hard. Her warm brown skin glistening with sweat. Her full breasts jiggling from the thrust of my cock into her wet slit. Her throaty voice screaming my name over and over. Then the dream had abruptly flipped and moved to her riding me like a stallion. Her toned thighs gripping my waist. Her pussy slick with our mingled juices lowering over my straining shaft. Her breasts pressed against my chest. The sounds of our labored breathing and the slapping of our bodies in perfect synchrony.

And most deplorable... her hot, pink tongue licking my neck

before her incisors struck, drinking my blood, feeding from me, while I pressed her mouth closer, begging her not to stop.

I grimaced. It would be a cold day in hell before I allowed a vampire to bite me. Even if the vampire was the sexy vixen Reason.

I despised vampires. Always had, always would. Besides, I'd never met a vampire who wasn't a cruel, calculating, bloodthirsty monster in sheep's clothing.

No, Reason wasn't worth my time. And I damn sure didn't have feelings for her.

My inner wolf whined, and I snarled aloud, trying to keep it in check. But my beast refused to stand down on its viewpoint. My wolf wanted Reason. And normally, what he wanted was what I wanted, but not this time.

Reason Orlov was on my Do Not Fuck list.

Swinging my legs over the leather sofa, I leaned forward, resting my elbows on my knees and my face in my hands. Scrubbing my fingers over my face, I stood up, glancing around my spacious apartment. My eyes drifted toward the cardboard boxes scrawled on in broad strokes with a felt-tip black marker. Years of Josie's personal possessions that I couldn't quite get up the fucking nerve to give away to charity.

Storming away from the sofa and toward my bedroom, my feet stopped before the side table with framed photos of Josie and me in military uniforms, holding weapons. Every time I saw the photos, it would bring back fond memories of the tomboy I had grown up with who followed me around, even into the military. Our friendship had turned into love, and when she'd found out she was pregnant, Josie had elected to get out of the military while I continued my career in the U.S. Special Forces.

Out of habit, my fingers ventured to the right, tracing over the US flag enshrined behind the glass top. Inside the case was a small photo of Josie. I sighed. Maybe Rip was right; it was finally time to let her go. I'd mourned her and my unborn child's deaths for years, even after I avenged their deaths by killing most of the vampires who had slaughtered them.

But revenge hadn't quieted the inner demons within me, nor had it brought me any closer to solace. And it damn sure hadn't been enough to help me move on with my life. Years later, I was still standing in an apartment devoid of life, except for the boxes stuffed with memories of Josie that I couldn't even bear to let go of. Or maybe I was just a sick fuck who loved to torture myself with the reminder that she and my unborn child were dead because of me.

But right now, it wasn't about the past. It was about moving forward into the future and someday hopefully finding happiness. The problem was I wasn't even sure I was done with mourning the past or ready to celebrate the possibilities of the future.

Drifting away from the table, I made my way into my enormous master suite. Except for the California-king bed, the room was barren and unadorned with sterile and dull white walls. The space was missing a woman's touch and vibrancy.

As I stripped off my clothes, my mind drifted to the vexing vampire Reason and how sexy she would look draped across my bed with her auburn hair spread across my pillows. My shaft stiffened, craving something I hadn't desired for the longest time. One woman to spend all my nights with, not the revolving door of women I'd fucked and discarded like disposable shavers just because I could.

Damn, I fucking resent the fact that Reason is making me almost feel again.

Scrubbing my fingers along my jaw, I stormed, naked, to my en-suite bathroom. Turning on the shower, I adjusted the temperature to cold before stepping beneath the showerhead, hoping the frigid water would get rid of my aching arousal. The jets beat against my body, but I was still at half-mast. Soaping myself up, my hand lingered on my erection. I couldn't go out tonight in this condition. I needed to stroke one out for sanity's sake.

Taking myself in my hand, I closed my eyes and tugged my thickness while the icy spray of the shower beat down on me like rain. I continued to rub my flesh. I thought about how Reason's glistening slit would taste against my tongue as I licked her hard little nub. Her hands would tightly clutch my head against her hot pussy…

My staff got even harder. A moan pushed past my lips.

"Holy fuck," I muttered.

I threw my head back, groaning, as I ejaculated until there was nothing left. Breathless, I opened my eyes. *Damn. If I came that hard from just imagining me doing those things to Reason, what would it be like if I touched her for real?*

I'd be lost.

My inner wolf growled, *Claim. Mate. Mine.*

Oh, fuck off. I'm not claiming her, I snapped back.

My wolf clawed at the edges of my mind, begging to come out and go find Reason. The struggle made my head pound. It took everything I had to fight the instinctual need tearing up my gut.

My wolf's obsession with Reason had to stop.

There was no way in hell I was going to claim a vampire… no matter how much my inner wolf wanted her.

Quickly, I washed my body and hair, rinsing away the shampoo and soap. Snatching one of my towels, I dried myself off before walking into my bedroom and then the large walk-in closet, coming back out with jeans and a black T-shirt. My jaw was tense as I pulled on my clothes and boots.

Leaving my quarters, I stepped into the elevator, which took me upstairs to Ryker Alfero's penthouse. The elevator opened directly into a grand foyer leading to a living and dining room with floor-to-ceiling windows and panoramic views of Central Park and the city. It was late and way past time for dinner, but the mouthwatering smell of sizzling steak wafted through the air. My stomach growled loudly, reminding me that, in all the chaos of Light's kidnapping, I'd missed lunch.

Walking into the penthouse and through the large living room, I glanced at the small gathering of weary wolf-shifters—Ryker, Rip, and Soar—my pack and friends, in the kitchen. Even though each team member had his own luxury apartment, it never failed that command central was always at our alpha's place. Over the years, our living quarters had turned into a quasi-fraternity house with the one elevator giving us unlimited access to each other's space. Despite the lack of privacy, Ryker, Rip, and Soar were my family, closer than flesh and blood. I'd take a bullet for any one of them, and I knew they'd do the same for me.

Rip was at the stove, searing steaks, when he abruptly turned to glower at me. "It's sleepyhead. I'm happy to see you finally got up," he finished with a wide smile.

Immediately going to the coffee pot, I grumbled under my breath, "Fuck off. I'm not in the mood. I've been working fucked-up leads, and I have absolutely nothing to get us any closer to finding Light."

After leaving Reason, I'd driven around Manhattan, paying visits to several of my regular and reliable informants. None of them had any info on the whereabouts of the Shadows or Light.

I poured a cup of coffee before glancing around the kitchen, taking stock of the pack. Soar was shoveling steak and mashed potatoes into his mouth like he hadn't eaten in days. And Ryker was sitting with a tension-filled pinched expression.

I leaned against the granite countertop, gulping my coffee.

Soar swallowed his mouthful of food and exclaimed, "You're not the only one who's been working hard, sifting through fucked-up intel, yet we"—he gestured between Rip, Ryker, and himself—"managed to get ourselves to our pack meeting on time."

"Soar, cut him some slack." Rip interrupted. "He was probably releasing some stress by jacking off while thinking about that smoking-hot hybrid vampire."

I leveled him with a stare. *Damn, the fucker knows me too well.* "Shut the fuck up, Rip." Pushing away from the counter, I slipped into the empty seat beside Ryker.

"Man, you're grouchy. You need to get laid… and fast," Rip countered while sliding a plate heavy with a huge steak and mashed potatoes toward me.

Giving Rip a warning stare, I dived into my plate. With this many shifters around, food tended to disappear quickly.

Soar leaned back in his chair with steepled fingers. "So what happened between you and the vampire?"

I swallowed my mouthful of food and placed my fork onto my plate, instantly losing my appetite. "Nothing." I cleared my throat. "I briefed her, like Knox had asked me to, and then dropped her home." Suddenly thirsty, I guzzled my coffee.

Soar examined me with way-too-wise eyes. "And?"

"And nothing," I snapped.

"What's your deal?" Soar countered. "I'm not asking if you fucked her. I'm asking if she's okay, given the fact that Light is missing. It's a lot to process. Maybe you should give her a call, find out how she's doing, and see if she's interested in crying on your shoulder." He gave me a devilish smile.

The asshole was fucking with me.

Rip snorted. "Yeah right. He's not going to do that shit. He'd rather mope around, pretending like he's not secretly lusting after her."

I slammed my cup onto the table. "I don't do vampires."

Rip grabbed a plate piled high with steak and potatoes, eyeballing me. "Yeah, that's why you were growling at anyone who even blinked at her the last time we were at Redemption. Bullshit." He walked over to the table and plopped down. "Here's some advice. Female vampires love a firm but gentle hand. Just give her your best alpha stare and tell her to get into your bed."

I scowled. "I'm not interested in Reason."

"Really?" Rip smiled with eager eyes. "If you don't want her, would you have a problem with me pursuing her? Because, man, that vampire is beautiful."

My eyes narrowed and my canines dropped.

"Would you all just shut up?" Ryker barked. "We have too much shit going on to be talking about Jackal's inability to seal the deal with Reason."

Rip and Soar eyed me and laughed.

Fuckers.

Ryker snarled. "My mate is still missing."

When he pressed his hands against the table, we all felt the immense power rolling off his body.

"And all I care about right now is getting her back," he remarked while calmly watching us. "Let's review what we definitely know and don't know so everyone's on the same damn page." He ran a hand through his hair.

The steady-thinking, stable Ryker was a fucking mess without his mate. And his disposition would only get worse if she died during this whole anarchy with the Shadows. I knew from firsthand experience that the depression would last forever and the bitterness would linger.

I'd learned it the hard way—the destruction and havoc that losing a true mate could cause. Losing my mate so many years ago had cut me deep, sending me to a dark and wild place. Only my pack's brotherhood and friendship had pulled me back from the brink of despair and death. And I was desperate to prevent Ryker from undergoing the same loss. Ryker needed us to help him find his other half, Light. Even a few hours apart for a newly mated wolf-shifter seemed like a lifetime.

"I've chased all my leads," I answered. "And I'm still no closer to finding out where the Shadows are hiding Light."

"Same here," Rip replied.

"I've got nothing," Soar declared. "It's like the Shadows disappeared from New York."

Ryker growled, "They're still here but just dug in somewhere like roaches. We need to lean on the right people to unearth them."

"Ryker," I started, deciding the best course of action was to tread carefully, "bro, our intel connections don't have anything, which leads me to believe that Baptiste probably took Light out of the country."

"No. She's still here... and real close," Ryker hissed. "I can feel her through our mate bond." His eyes flashed, his feral power rolling off him, but he quickly reined it in.

I sighed heavily, not sure if Ryker's belief was wishful thinking or fact. He was a fucking ticking time bomb waiting to explode. That was the exact reason Others were wary of him, especially since the goddess of death had appointed him as the bearer of the Sword of Souls with the full power and authority to take or give life.

"Okay then, Ryker, what's next?" Rip asked. "Light's our alpha female, and you know we'll fight to the death to get her back, but we're not addressing the elephant in the room. You've got more than Light to be concerned about."

I nodded in agreement. "There's a real clusterfuck developing in New York. Others are on the verge of war—again."

When Ryker had become head of the Other Council, he'd pledged to unite the wolf-shifters and bring peace to New York. A pledge was the only reason there had been a truce between Others and his pack. Now, this truce had been broken by a series of shifter and vampire deaths. All orchestrated by the Shadows.

Soar stared pensively. "Adding to the bullshit, my informants told me tonight that Orlov had announced to his coven that he'd still abide by the temporary truce between his coven and the shifters. But he'd not be entering into permanent truce talks with Ryker and the rest of the shifters until he knew the truth behind the death of his second-in-command, Dimitri, and the intentions of the shifters to eradicate the Shadows."

My mouth flopped open and then snapped closed. *What the hell? No permanent truce talks?*

An uncomfortable sensation settled over me like a scratchy wool sweater. Orlov's decision to pause permanent truce talks would crumble all of Ryker's hard work to dust.

I respected Ryker—not just because he was my alpha, but also because I'd witnessed personally his actions to broker peace between shifters and vampires. Ryker had defied the naysayers when the goddess of death appointed him the leader of the Other Council, promising the shifters—tigers, lions, wolves, dragons, and bears—a new beginning. A new start that included cleaning up years of shifter wars started by his out-of-control father. But now that the Shadows had kidnapped his mate, all his time would be spent trying to locate her—and rightly so, since finding his mate came first. Eventually, Ryker would become stretched thin between his battle to get his mate back and his obligations as leader of the Other Council.

Shit, he's between a rock and a hard place.

Ryker's face was grim when he stated, "I wouldn't put stock in what Orlov told his coven. It's all smoke and mirrors. I know for a fact he's hedging his bets on who's going to come out the victor in my impending war against the Shadows."

"Fact?" Soar asked.

Ryker nodded. "Orlov called me the same time Soar said his informants told him different and offered his help with getting Light back."

I snorted. "Bullshit. How?"

Ryker's eyes roamed to each of us. "Baptiste contacted Orlov and offered him a deal. If Orlov joins forces with the Shadows to destroy the shifters, when the war is over, Baptiste will give him half of the territories won."

"Well, it's official," I growled. "The avalanche of shit is mounting."

Rip stared at Ryker like he'd lost his ever-loving mind. "And exactly how is Orlov's partnership with the Shadows a win for us?"

Ryker frowned. "Orlov now has a direct line of communication with Baptiste. We don't. If Orlov tricks Baptiste into believing they have an alliance, sooner or later, Baptiste will slip up and disclose to him where he's holding Light."

Rip shook his head. "I don't like this shit."

"I don't either," Soar grunted.

I suspiciously eyed Ryker. "And what does Orlov get for bestowing you with this magnanimous favor of snitching on Baptiste?"

"He wants me to arrange a meeting for him with the goddess of death," Ryker answered.

"What?" Rip, Soar, and I yelled in unison.

To Others, the goddess of death was the equivalent of the Grim Reaper. Shifter folklore talked of seeing the goddess riding her stallion across the battlefield while collecting souls for enslavement.

"That shit is straight up suicide," I sneered.

Not that I gave a shit about a world minus Oskar Orlov. His conniving manipulation had caused the deaths of many innocent Others, and he deserved everything he had coming to him. But I did care about Reason. I knew her father's demise would devastate her.

"You think?" Ryker spit sarcastically. "But that's Orlov's funeral. All I want is my mate back. So I'll set up the meeting with the goddess once he fulfills his end of the bargain."

Soar scoffed. "You can't trust Orlov. No one can. He's a backstabbing prick."

Ryker scowled. "Don't you think I know that shit? That's why my deal with him expressly states that any information or help he provides has to result in Light being physically in my possession before I arrange his meeting with the goddess."

"I don't get this shit. What does he want from the goddess?" Rip inquired.

"Don't know," Ryker grumbled, "and I don't care. I just want Light back."

"And what if the goddess refuses to meet with Orlov?" I asked.

Ryker remarked, "Believe me, she won't. In fact, I think she'll get perverse pleasure in meeting him. The woman has a sick fascination with vampires. She collects them as her minions and sexual pets."

"Damn!" Rip exclaimed. "The woman sounds like my type of girl. When can I meet her?" He grinned.

"Never," Ryker gritted out. "She's pure evil wrapped in a body and face of a siren."

Soar's cell beeped. As he slid a finger across it, he smiled. "Just in time. This is the intel I've been waiting on." He frowned. "Shit. Three sightings of the Shadows."

"How reliable is the source?" Ryker asked.

"Very," Soar stated. "Let's go." He tapped out a text, and everyone's cell beeped. "Those are the locations. I'll take the first, and you guys can figure out how you want to divide the rest."

Everyone started to scoot back from the table when Ryker's cell rang.

"Vivica?" he answered. "Slow down. I can't understand a fucking thing you're saying." He paced back and forth. "The Shadows are at Redemption?" His jaw tightened. "Okay, okay. Don't panic. Just keep them there." He ended the call, putting his cell into his pocket. "The Shadows are partying at Redemption. What the hell is going on? We've gone from no sightings to several, just like that."

"I don't like this shit," Rip commented. "Sounds like they're fucking with our heads."

"I agree," I replied. "But we've got to move on all leads. I'll take Redemption."

I stormed over to the elevator when a feeling of dread raced through my body. A response that was always a warning of bad things to come.

"Men," I shouted over my shoulder, "watch your backs tonight! I've got a funny hunch that shit's about to get real dangerous."

❦ 3 ❦

REASON

*J*ESUS. *All that fucking blood.*

Just thinking about the violence that had taken place at tonight's Blood Rite almost kicked in my gag reflex… again.

I shuddered at the memory of Dad's enforcers rushing into the ballroom with Serena, a beautiful pale, waif-thin woman, cuffed at the wrists. The crowd had parted, making way for them to approach the dais where Dad and I sat on our thrones. The enforcers had bowed their heads in respect, but Serena had not. I didn't blame her, given the circumstances for her presence. We hadn't run in the same social circles, but I'd made it my business to learn all about her when Dad decided to call the coven together tonight. Like me, Serena had been a young vampire who lived her life more in the human world than the vampire world. And that was what had gotten Serena in the hot mess tonight. She had fallen in love with a human and broken the most sacred vampire covenant for him. Now, Serena would be immortalized as the vampire stupid enough to give her blood to a human, forfeiting her life.

Without remorse, cocky Stefan had toyed with Serena and her human mate a bit before swiftly ending their lives.

"I can't believe Stefan cut off their damn heads," I whispered aloud to myself while swerving through Manhattan traffic. "Barbaric."

The Blood Rite ceremony was an archaic tradition encased in a facade of civility to show all vampires that there were dire consequences for breaking covenant laws. And even though I deplored the Blood Rite practice, I understood the need for it. The world was dangerous for vampires, and to offer our blood to humans who didn't understand or respect the pure power it contained was asking for trouble. The vampires' existence could easily be discovered, and given the history of humans, we would be hunted and experimented on just so they could exploit the properties within the vampire bloodline.

A yellow cab cut me off, causing me to hit my brakes hard.

"Asshole drivers!" I yelled while beeping my horn like a lunatic.

Pulling around the cab, I threw the driver the bird before speeding off. Granted, I was in a fucked-up mood after racing home from the Blood Rite and stripping off my gown to rid myself of the stench of blood. Frankly, I should've called it a night and just stayed home. But the emptiness of my townhouse had driven me crazy. So I had thrown on some clothes and decided to go to the one place that had always been my solace and savior. The office. Being deep in work would keep me from dwelling on the lonely void of my nonexistent personal and social life.

As I veered through traffic, my cell rang. Smoothly, I tapped the button on my console, allowing the call to permeate the confines of my vehicle.

"Hey, Storm," I answered, annoyed by a car that had made a turn in front of me without putting on its signal indicator. "Anything new on Light?"

My heart raced with anxiety as I thought about the deal I'd made with the devil—Dad—at the Blood Rite. For his agreement to pledge his enforcers and connections to help Ryker find Light, I had consented to take Stefan as my consort by marrying him. But that was the sacrifice I was willing to make. Light needed my help. To make matters worse, Dad had given me a deadline of thirty days to plan the wedding and get married.

"Yes." Storm's voice was filled with excitement. "The pack found several credible leads on the whereabouts of the Shadows. Reason, we're so close to finding her. I can feel it."

I breathed a sigh of relief. "Thank God."

"I just can't believe the Shadows would be partying at Redemption of all places."

"Redemption?" My hands tightened around the steering wheel. "That's odd." An uncomfortable sensation settled over me.

Redemption was frequented by key players in the New York Other circle. Redemption was more of a VIP restaurant visited by the rich-and-famous Others and humans, with a long waiting list. The difference between Vivica's restaurant and other celebrity-frequented restaurants was everyone who went there wanted their privacy because of the type of acts that took place there. Sexual acts were orchestrated on a stage for all to see while patrons ate, watched, and had their own personal shows in their secluded booths, given the proper motivation.

"Very," Storm replied. "According to Knox, Ryker doesn't want to leave any stone unturned, so they're going to check out the Redemption tip anyway."

Veering off route to the office, I headed toward Redemption. Something wasn't right. I felt it in my bones. "And talking about Ryker"—I cleared my throat, struggling with how to tell Storm about what my dad had announced at the Blood Rite—"my father has decided not to enter into permanent truce talks with Ryker and the rest of the shifters until he knows the truth behind the death of Dimitri."

"What the hell? No permanent truce talks?"

"None," I replied.

"Oh God. This is not good. Reason, I've got to go. I need to talk to Knox and figure out what the hell is going on." She paused. "I'll give you a call if I hear anything else about their progress with finding Light."

"Okay. Talk to you soon."

Our call ended, and I wasted no time in speeding through Manhattan. Finally reaching my destination, I parked in the alleyway and hopped out of my SUV. As I made my way to the front, my eyes darted around at the guests walking up to the entrance that was blocked by two huge security guards.

I could count on one hand the number of times I'd come to Redemption. It just wasn't my thing to be around so many Others, but tonight, I had a strange feeling that here was exactly where I needed to be.

When I approached the entrance, a well-toned young man dressed in a well-cut suit bowed. "Welcome, Princess Orlov," he greeted as the guards opened the doors and scurried out of the way.

I nodded in acknowledgement. "What's the theme tonight?"

I hoped it wasn't kink night. I wasn't in the mood to witness the hottest sexcapade in town. Vivica loved throwing invite-only kink parties several times a year for her VIP vampire clients. The parties gave her vampire clients the opportunity to get blood from Others and humans who wanted to walk on the wild side and liked to be bitten and have sex.

"It's consort night," he replied.

I stepped through the entry and into a huge space. Redemption was packed, and the party was in full swing. The heavy pounding of the music reverberated throughout the dimly lit room. The expensively designed restaurant transformed into a club on the entire first floor. Rich fabric was draped across the ceiling. The outer perimeter of the dance floor had several booths with high backs and wide sides facing away from the dance floor, obstructing the view of any voyeurs. Suddenly, some of the booths swung to face the dance floor, giving me full view of the guests attired in extremely provocative clothing—from latex to corsets to skintight leather. Most everyone had a glass of champagne, and I was happy there were no obvious goblets of blood.

I walked around the perimeter of Redemption, searching for Vivica. Scanning the area, I skidded to a stop, almost bumping into the couple swaying in place. The man's arms were protectively wrapped around the woman, cradling her, and I was fascinated. The woman pulled away from his neck, licked the lingering blood glistening on her lips, and raised an adoring gaze to his. For a split second, envy slithered through my veins at the obvious love and happiness they had for each other.

The female vampire stuck her finger into her mouth and then bit it, and I saw blood glinting in the light. The vampire's gaze never left her lover's as his mouth opened promptly, greedily sucking her finger. His cheeks hollowed out as he slurped on her hard. His eyes closed again as he pulled her hand from his mouth and eagerly kissed her, his hands frantically lifting the hem of her leather dress until her creamy thighs were exposed. The vampire woman laughed as he pushed her into the shadows.

"Reason?" a voice I instantly recognized called.

My eyes focused on the tall, pale redhead making a beeline toward me.

"What are you doing here?" she asked, pulling me in for a quick hug before stepping back.

"Hi, Vivica."

Vivica nearly spilled out of an eye-popping, body-hugging black jumpsuit that revealed her ample cleavage. She'd teamed her ensemble with a pair of strappy black stilettos and a few gold bracelets and rings for added sparkle.

"What? I can't drop by and have a drink at my aunt's club?"

Vivica and I weren't related, but she'd been my father's close friend for so long that she'd become part of my dysfunctional family.

She frowned. "Not tonight. Now go home, young lady." She

started ushering me toward the entrance. "Trouble is brewing tonight, and I don't want you anywhere near it."

I stubbornly pulled away and stared at her. "So it's true. The Shadows are here."

"Yes. The fuckers just walked in and started partying like rock stars."

Both of our eyes caught Jacque, her normally cool-as-a-cucumber assistant, beckoning Vivica over from the corner of the room. He appeared decidedly rumpled and frazzled.

"What happened to him?" I asked.

She rolled her eyes. "The Shadows. They roughed him up a bit when he told them they weren't on the guest list." She sighed heavily. "It's like there's a full moon tonight. Anything and everything that could go fucking wrong tonight has."

I cocked my head to the side. "Where are Victor and Alexandro?"

It was highly unusual for Vivica to be without her two huge consorts, who were always protectively hovering by her sides.

"Oskar sent them on some top-secret assignment." She pursed her lips. "They won't be back until next week."

Jacque was waving frantically at her.

"Stay put. I'll be right back." She kissed me hard on the cheek before practically gliding across the floor.

I watched Jacque, who had now turned beet red, jab a finger in the direction of a group of rowdy men in a corner booth with multiple bottles of alcohol littering their table. Vivica patted his arm, as if trying to calm him down. I deduced the group of men was a part of the Shadows because they damn sure didn't look like the normal clientele that patronized Redemption. No, these men were unrefined, bawdy, and stuck out like sore thumbs. I frowned. And I got the sense they were trying way too hard not to fit into the scene, as if they were attempting to be memorable to everyone around them.

This was... strange.

As I was caught up in my musings, unexpectedly, a shiver

went down my spine, as if I had been blasted with frigid air. Someone was watching me. My body trembled with unease, and my gaze swiveled around, drawn to the only man on earth who simultaneously made my sex clench with lust and stomach roll with distaste—Jackal.

He sauntered toward me with fire in his eyes, looking scrumptious in dark jeans and a black T-shirt that stretched across his muscled wide chest. I refused to move as his eyes locked on me, trapping me to the spot, as he stood before me.

Jackal's eyes narrowed, and his nostrils flared. "What are you doing here?"

I let out a breath I didn't know I'd been holding. "No hello? Where are your manners, shifter?"

He silently stared at me. His large frame would intimidate anyone, but I refused to be cowed by him.

I raised my chin in a gesture of defiance and met his gaze. "What I'm doing here is none of your damn business, Jackal. Now go away. You're scaring away all the eligible man candy interested in fucking me senseless."

His mouth compressed into a thin line.

With an aggrieved sigh, I answered, "Relax, shifter. I'm here to grab a drink."

"Well, you need to drink up and then hustle your ass out of here. There's a dangerous crowd in here tonight." His gaze flicked to the corner of the room.

"Thanks for the concern, wolf. But I'm a big girl, and I can take care of myself."

He inched closer. "Can you now?" He reached out and grazed the side of my cheek with the back of his hand.

Jesus, he smelled delicious... like cedar and sandalwood swirled together into an alluring, perfect combination.

"Yes, I can." My clit thumped against my panties as an erotic image flashed through my mind... me on all fours and those big hands all over my body while he fucked me from behind.

A soft growl left Jackal's lips when my tongue snaked out to wet my lips.

This thing between us had to stop. I'd allowed him to burrow under my skin like a tick, and that wasn't good for either of us.

The pulse along his jaw jumped like mad. "Get the fuck out of here, Reason. The Shadows are here, and things are about to get real ugly in a minute." He turned on his heels, storming away toward Vivica.

I watched as they talked briefly before Vivica nodded over at the group of rowdy men—the Shadows. There was a flurry of movement when several of the Shadows suddenly stood up, walking away toward the back exit.

Jackal followed.

My body tensed. An ominous feeling clouded my head. Something was terribly wrong.

I pushed through the dance floor in pursuit of Jackal. It was as if my body were on autopilot. Emotions I'd never felt before —desperation, fear, and dread—drove me to pursue him. The emotions were cloying, like cheap perfume.

I felt feverish, alert, and sick to my stomach.

Stepping out of the exit door into the dimly lit alleyway, I heard a rustle to the right, down a ways. The sight of Jackal fighting the Shadows jolted me.

He was outnumbered but holding them off with a series of wicked-looking kicks and punches that sent his attackers sprawling in waves to the ground. But in a flurry of movement, the tide turned on Jackal as the men whipped out shiny blades and started swinging and slashing against his body. Jackal grunted and then crashed to the ground. The Shadows scattered and fled the scene.

My heart raced with fear. Jackal wasn't moving, lying in a pool of his own blood. The smell and sight of the blood made me queasy, but I was determined to move forward. I crept closer to see how bad his injuries were. Crouching down, I eyed his numerous stab wounds, which were too many to count. Even worse, it didn't seem like he was healing. Touching his pulse, I felt nothing. He wasn't breathing, and his skin was pale and ice cold.

My stomach clenched. He was dead.

No, I can't lose him. No, I fucking refuse to lose him.

Save him, a voice whispered in my head.

No, I couldn't. I shouldn't. It is strictly forbidden.

I sat back on my heels, staring at his prone body. Tears pricked my eyes as I felt the loss of a man I didn't even know that well. I wiped my cheeks. It was done, and I had to get out of here.

Save him now, the voice in my head hissed with more urgency. *He's not dead. He can be saved.*

Reaching down, I felt his pulse again. It was faint but there. This was the fork-in-the-road decision, and once made, there would be no going back. Pushing up my sleeve, I brought my wrist to my lips, biting down hard. Searing pain raced up my arm. Blood dripped from the wound. Driven by a primal force I didn't even understand, I pressed my wrist against his pale lips, feeding him my blood.

"Drink," I whispered.

Nothing happened.

Frankly, I hadn't expected it to. I was a hybrid and didn't have the blood-saving properties that pure-blooded vampires did, but I was desperate. Widening his mouth, I dripped more blood inside, letting it coat his tongue. I jumped when I felt his lips move and his tongue lick against my wrist. My pussy pulsed from the contact. The strangeness of him drinking from me was different and somewhat sensual.

Suddenly, he coughed and then moaned. And then the gravity of what I'd done hit me like a ton of bricks. It was against the vampire covenant to give a non-vampire blood. The punishment was death.

Jackal groaned. The color of his skin was no longer lifeless, but his eyes were still closed. I heard the familiar squeak of

Redemption's exit door and quickly yanked my wrist away from Jackal's lips.

Vivica came running toward me with wild eyes. She stared at me with her mouth hanging open before demanding, "Reason? What the fuck did you do?"

I scrambled to my feet. "Nothing," I mumbled, folding my arms across my chest.

"Bullshit," she spit, glaring at my bleeding wrist. "You fed him your blood. What the hell were you thinking?"

"He was dying," I replied defensively. "I didn't think. I just did."

Vivica's face crumbled into ultimate panic. "Oh God. I can't even think right now." She leaned over with her hands on her knees, hyperventilating. "Orlov is going to kill me, and it's going to be a slow, painful death."

I anxiously glanced around the alleyway. Sooner or later, people would stream out of Redemption, and I needed to get Jackal out of here. "Vivica, we have to move him."

"This is utter madness," she retorted. "No. Let's go," she ordered, snatching my hand, trying to drag me away.

I didn't budge. "No. I'm not leaving Jackal on the fucking ground like garbage."

Vivica eyed me like she wanted to choke me. "Jesus, Reason. What the fuck is wrong with you? You just committed the greatest sin—thou shall not give a non-vampire blood."

"What I did cannot be undone." I tapped my foot. "So help me get him into my SUV and forget everything you saw here."

She pursed her pouty lips. "Okay. Give me a minute to formulate my response." She paused dramatically. "That would be a resounding *hell no!*" She gawked at me like I was crazy.

I arched a brow. "Why not?"

She glared at me. "Are you fucking kidding me right now? Your father would have my ass if he found out I helped cover this shit up." She shook her head. "No, I'm not doing it. Do you have any idea what you just did? In one fell swoop, you put my business, my consorts, and me in jeopardy. My friendship with Orlov won't mean anything once he finds out about this blood shit."

"That is even more motivation for you to help me clean this mess up."

I knew I was being unreasonable, but I didn't care. I needed help, and Vivica was the only one who could provide it right now.

"No," Vivica snapped. "We're going to call Ryker and tell him to hustle his ass over here to pick up his friend."

I shook my head. "Not a good idea. I need to take Jackal to my house for observation. I'm not sure how his body is going to respond to vampire blood."

"This is fucked up, Reason. I'm smack dab in a clusterfuck you created."

"And I'm sorry for putting you in this awkward position." I really was. "But I'm not leaving Jackal unconscious in a fucking alleyway. That shit is cruel. Now... help me, Vivica." I touched her shoulder. "Please."

Her eyes widened. "Shit, you must really like this wolf-shifter." She sighed heavily. "Okay. But once we're done..." She trailed off, scrutinizing me. "We will not ever talk about what we did here to anyone."

"Got it," I answered impatiently. "Let's get to it."

We were wasting way too much time talking. I glanced at my vehicle parked at the other end of the alleyway. Between the two of us and some vampire strength, we could get him there. I reached into my pocket and pulled out my key fob, pressing it to unlock all doors before shoving it back into my pocket. Then we both crouched down, each grabbing an arm, hefting Jackal up. His head dropped forward, but he didn't make a sound as we dragged him toward my automobile.

"Hold on," I huffed. "Prop him against the door while I open the back."

Efficiently, we shoved him against the SUV while I opened the back door.

"Now."

We rolled him sideways, letting his body's momentum drop him into the backseat. Still, not a sound came out of Jackal. Tucking his long, muscular legs inside, I slammed the door and sagged against it. Breathing heavily, I wiped my hand across my sweaty forehead.

"Jesus, the shifter is nothing but solid muscle," Vivica commented before opening the passenger's door.

"What are you doing, Vivica?"

"Going home with you. How else are you going to be able to lug his ass inside?" she commented before tiredly getting in.

Quickly, I ran around to the driver's door and hopped in. Turning on the vehicle, I reversed out of the alleyway with fingers gripping the wheel like a life preserver. Jackal growled low in his throat and then went silent.

As I raced through the darkness, the gravity of what I'd just done cloaked me like a scratchy wool sweater. And I knew with everything in me that I was truly fucked.

❧ 4 ☙

REASON

It was a struggle, but Vivica and I got Jackal into my Manhattan townhouse and then into my master bedroom.

I pointed to the bed. "Drop him."

Simultaneously, we released our hold on him, allowing him to fall against the mattress.

"Jesus, he's a bloody mess." Vivica glared down at him. "They really fucked him up. He should be dead."

I stood, staring at Jackal sprawled across my king-size bed. He was barely breathing and drenched in blood. She was right. Jackal shouldn't be alive right now. He had multiple stab wounds, and some of the cuts looked deep.

"His cuts aren't closing." Vivica frowned. "I thought shifters healed fast."

"I think they have to shift from human to their animal form for the healing process to start. He needs his animal right now." I bit my bottom lip. It was troublesome that his wolf hadn't appeared to help him with the healing process.

"Come on, Jackal." Vivica reached down and poked him with a finger like he was some horrible experiment gone wrong. "Shift."

"Don't do that," I snapped. Vivica touching him made me

feel like ripping her skin off and wearing it like a fur coat. "You can leave now. I got it from here."

"Oh, I see." She smirked. "Don't want me touching your wolf-shifter, huh?"

"He's not my wolf-shifter," I retorted while rubbing my brow to ward off a headache.

"Yeah right." Vivica winked at me. "I really don't blame you. Even for a shifter, he's smoking hot. I mean, Jesus, look at his body."

"Okay, that's it. Good-bye, Vivica." I pushed her out of my bedroom and down the hallway. Opening the front door, I gestured for her to get moving.

Her eyebrows drew together. "I really don't think it's wise for me to leave you with that shifter. He's injured, and he could lash out at you."

The truth of the matter was I wasn't even sure he'd make it through the night. "Don't worry about me. I can handle Jackal."

Vivica stood silently, biting her full bottom lip.

I leaned forward and quickly kissed her cheek before saying, "Thank you for having my back tonight. It truly means the world to me."

Vivica shrugged. "We're family."

"It's late. Now get out." I shoved her over the threshold.

"Okay, okay. I'm going." She trotted down the front stairs and then stopped, glancing over her shoulder at me. "Call me first thing in the morning. I'm dying to know how this shifter-versus-vampire reality show ends."

"Probably badly," I mumbled before shutting the door and swaying back to the bedroom.

Jackal was still lying in the position I'd left him in. *Now what?* I paced back and forth with my mind buzzing. *Why the hell did I give him my blood?*

"Because I'm an idiot; that's why," I scolded aloud. "Shit, Dad's going to fucking kill me."

I was practically pulling out my hair now, feeling the full

weight of my actions. I didn't need this shit at the moment. My life was complicated enough.

Stopping beside the bed, I glared down at Jackal, the bane of my existence. The man whom I'd betrayed Dad's trust for was just lying there without a damn care in the world—besides barely breathing.

I didn't understand. Vampire blood should have saved him immediately—or at least I'd thought it would have. *But what the hell do I know?* I was just a hybrid vampire and a novice at feeding anyone blood.

"First things first," I said, heading over to the bathroom.

Once inside, I grabbed some towels and dampened several washcloths. Walking back over to the bed, I dropped everything onto the nightstand and pulled off Jackal's shitkicker boots, letting them fall onto the floor with a loud thud. Reaching down, I unzipped his jeans and nearly swallowed my tongue.

"Oh God. He's commando."

Even in its relaxed state, his member was freaking huge.

"Reason, focus. Keep your mind off the man's cock."

Gritting my teeth, I yanked off his jeans and then his T-shirt. Taking a damp washcloth, I started wiping off all the blood coating his body. I was resolute in my goal to get through this cleansing without getting distracted by Jackal's naked, muscular body.

It didn't take long before focus turned into failure. The man was gorgeous, impossibly so, with rippling muscles and a powerful torso. His body, from chest to wrist, was a wonderland of beautifully composed Japanese tattoos and other beast-themed ink.

My eyes roamed over his glorious body from his wide chest to the tantalizing line arrowed over his well-defined six-pack stomach. My eyes drifted down to the jet-black hair at the apex of his mammoth toned thighs. And lying there was the most magnificent, biggest cock I'd ever seen. It was absolute perfection.

I continued to clean his wounds, which were healing but way too slowly. At this rate, I wasn't sure Jackal would make it. He needed to shift into his wolf to heal himself, but he was knocked out.

By the time I was done with Jackal, I was exhausted, and my clothes were freaking disheveled and covered with his blood.

Quickly moving to my linen closet, I pulled out a blanket, carrying it back to the bed to cover him with it.

"Done!" I exclaimed with finality.

Now it was time for me to clean up and get some sleep. Striding over to the bathroom, I peeled off my blood-soaked clothes. Stepping into the shower, letting the water sweep away the grime, I soaped up and then washed my hair but didn't linger. I was exhausted and needed a couple hours of sleep to cope with the mayhem that would be awaiting me in the morning when Jackal woke up.

Stepping out of the shower, I quickly dried off and slipped into boy-cut shorts and a tank top. Yawning, I slowly made my way out of the bathroom, only to see that the blanket had shifted off Jackal, revealing his manhood that was now semierect.

I blinked. "Jesus, it's an anaconda."

My pussy fluttered with small pulses. Under different circumstances—like way less stressful and deadly circumstances—I wouldn't mind staring at his hard-on for hours, like a piece of fine art in a museum. But now all I could think about was covering the monster and getting some well-deserved rest. The only way I'd be able to figure out how the hell I was going to fix this Jackal situation was on a good night's sleep.

Sighing heavily, I pulled the blanket over him. He was burning up. I could feel heat radiating from his skin. I pressed my fingers to his forehead to check his temperature. I nearly jumped out of my skin when his eyelids snapped open. Cloudy apple-green eyes stared up at me. Lightning fast, he wrapped his callused fingers around my wrist and flipped me onto the bed, pinning me beneath him.

Jesus, I'm fucked.

I tried to push his limbs off, but the more I shoved, the more determined he seemed to cling to me. His rod was hard and hot on my stomach.

"Jackal, get the hell off me."

Ignoring me, he stuck his nose into my neck. "You smell delicious." His voice was husky and filled with sleep as he loudly sniffed me. "I wonder if you taste just as good as you smell." Wasting no time, his mouth closed over the delicate skin on my neck before his rough tongue licked, and he nibbled me like a man on a mission.

And I loved it.

"No, no, no," I whispered. "Not good." Reaching up, I dug my fingers into his hair to pull him away.

His growl was almost feral in nature.

"Mate. Claim. Mine." His voice was a velvet whisper before his mouth latched onto my neck like a dog with a bone, but not breaking my skin.

My body overrode the warning in my head. Splaying my fingers against his head, I relaxed, enjoying the sensation of his lips pressed against me. I wondered what it would be like to have him fucking me, to have his lips roaming over every inch of my heated flesh before his head dipped between my legs.

"Oh, Josie," Jackal huskily whispered with reverence.

Oh, hell no. My body stiffened. *Who the fuck is Josie?*

❦   5   ❦

JACKAL

THERE WAS an annoying dull pain in my head as I flipped over onto my stomach. Pressing my nose into the pillow, I inhaled the lingering, familiar sultry aroma of vanilla, lavender, and citrus with soft floral, reminding me of Reason.

Damn, that's sexy.

Wait... What the fuck?

I jolted awake, lying tangled in a blanket on a king-size bed, sweating profusely. Scrambling to sit up, I tried to clear my sleep-fogged brain.

Where am I?

My inner beast growled while prowling back and forth, agitated. I smelled Reason all over this room. My cock jerked as the alluring scent floated up my nostrils. It was sensual and intoxicating. Just like the woman the scent had come from.

Pressing my back against the upholstered headboard, I just sat there, blinking at the bright sunlight streaming across the massive foreign bedroom. The last thing I remembered was fighting the Shadows in the alleyway behind Redemption... and I had given the fuckers a run for their money.

But how the hell did I get here?

Pushing away the blanket, I swung my legs over the edge of

49

bed, scanning the spacious bedroom with floor-to-ceiling windows. The decor was decidedly feminine and tasteful. On the dressing table was a photo of a beautiful woman with dark-brown skin, cradling a baby in her arms. The woman looked like a replica of Reason, only older.

When I heard approaching soft strikes of feet hitting the floor, my head snapped in the direction of the closed door.

"Reason, play it cool," I heard Reason whisper.

What the fuck? My hearing was good, but not this good.

The bed dipped when I eased myself onto my feet. The door swung open, with Reason standing on the threshold, looking refreshed and gorgeous, carrying folded clothes. My wolf stood at attention, practically salivating. My manhood instantly got hard, as it always did when I saw the damn vampire.

She bit her plump bottom lip as my eyes traveled from the top of her head and down her curvy body.

One thing I knew for certain; she was one of the most stunning women I'd ever laid eyes on. Tall and voluptuous with curves that cried out to be caressed and fucked. Tight jeans accentuated her figure, and a body-hugging black tank top embraced her tempting tits. Her hair cascaded to her shoulders, and her face was freshly scrubbed and makeup-free. She had the face of an exotic goddess. I memorized her every feature—from her rich brown skin to her tilt-tipped nose and full bow-shaped lips.

I ran a hand through my sleep-tousled hair. "Good morning, Reason," I drawled huskily, making no attempt to conceal my straining erection.

"Good morning, Jackal." She almost purred her words while tossing her long auburn hair.

I could tell she'd just washed her hair this morning from the damp strands sticking together between the dried. My stomach tightened. My eyesight was more acute than ever. Something wasn't right.

Reason quirked a brow in my direction. "Are you done eye-fucking me, shifter?"

My eyes locked with hers. "Not quite." I paused. "Why don't you turn around, place your hands on the wall, and pretend you're under arrest? I want to check out that sweet ass of yours." My cock grew hard at the mere thought.

She frowned. "I hate to disappoint you, wolfie, but that shit is not happening—ever," she snapped before walking forward and dropping the folded clothes in her hands onto the bed.

I could smell her arousal, and the delicious scent almost made me slam her to the floor and fuck her like a recently released prisoner.

Reason's eyes were cold when she continued. "Now get dressed and get the fuck out of my house before my father's enforcers stop by for their daily check on me." She stepped back and eyed me. "I washed your clothes. They're a little worse for wear with the holes and rips, but I got most of the blood out." She pointed over to the far end of the room. "My bathroom is over there. I also called Ryker and told him where you were. He's sending someone over to get you."

My brows knitted. She was all business, like she was checking items off a list. Her perfunctory manner fucking irked me. I had no intention of being dismissed by her that easily. I widened my stance, and my erection bobbed against my stomach. Reason hissed as her eyes locked on to my length.

My inner wolf pranced about like a show horse, chanting, *Hey! Look at me! Look at me!*

"Eyes up here, vampire," I ordered.

"Why?" She batted her eyelashes, almost comically. "When the view down there is just so much better."

"Smartass." My lips twisted into a smirk.

"That I am." Her lips tilted into a brief small smile.

My heart thumped hard in my chest. Damn, I loved her sassy take-no-shit attitude. But there was one important matter at hand.

"Reason, what am I doing here?" I suspiciously eyed her.

"That's a long and complicated story. The short answer is I saved your ass after those men—" She spoke nonchalantly.

"The Shadows," I cut in.

"Yes, the Shadows. Well, they ambushed you in the alley last night. You were hurt. Pretty bad, I might add." She fidgeted.

I smelled a strong whiff of anxiousness intermixing with her alluring scent. Not giving her a chance to recover, I pinned her under a hard glare. "And?"

"And we'll talk more about it when you're done with your shower." She turned on her heel, practically running out of the bedroom.

I ran a hand over my chin. My sexy vampire was hiding something, and I was determined to find out what.

6

REASON

LEANING AGAINST MY GRANITE COUNTER, I sipped espresso while staring at the multiple food platters spread across the counter, piled high with scrambled eggs, pancakes, biscuits, bacon, ham, sausages, and more sausages. Cooking was what I did to release anxiety and stress. And waiting for Jackal to finally wake up had left me with way too many hours to indulge in my favorite pastime.

Dammit! I'd had a perfectly good plan this morning. Wake him the hell up and quickly shove him out of my townhouse. But what I hadn't planned on was stepping into my bedroom, only to find the freak of nature awake and naked with his morning hard-on on full display and practically waving, as if saying, *Hi, and good morning to you*.

And what the hell was up with his flirting with me? I fucking hated Jackal's damn mixed signals. *Is he interested in me? Or is he just fucking with me?* I couldn't get a clear read on him.

Not that it even mattered, especially after he'd dropped the Josie bomb on me last night. Immediately after that bullshit, I'd tried to push him off, but I'd been unsuccessful. I was no match for the heavy-limbed Jackal. I'd ended up lying prone with his face nestled in my neck while he snored loudly. Hours later, when he'd rolled over while still sleeping, I'd scrambled off the bed and escaped into my guestroom to get some shut-eye. Not that I'd gotten any rest. Nope. I'd just lain there, staring at the ceiling, fuming, and asking myself a ton of questions that I didn't have the damn answers for.

Who is Josie? A lover? An ex-girlfriend? An exotic dancer at his favorite strip club? And most importantly, what type of man calls another woman's name in the current woman's bed?

My doorbell rang with short, sharp, urgent bursts, jolting me out of my thoughts. Finally, Ryker was here to take away my one source of stress—Jackal. Prowling over to the door with anxiousness and anticipation balled up in the pit of my stomach, I peered through the peephole. Standing at my door was a woman with sleek black tresses left loose around her shoulders and eyes shielded with aviators.

Oh shit. Not good.

I opened it. "What are you doing here, Demi?" I inquired.

Demi whipped off her sunglasses, smiling impishly. "Hello to you, too." She kissed my cheek before swaying in with a designer bag on her shoulder and a woven basket dangling on the crook of her arm. "Where is he?" Her eyes darted around.

"Who's *he?*" I slammed the door and locked it.

Demi arched a well-groomed brow. "Last night, I had a vision of some guy getting his ass handed to him. He was muscular, hot, and alphalicious, but surprisingly, he did not make my vajayjay quiver."

My mouth dropped open and then closed. *Oh God. She had a psychic vision about Jackal.*

She handed me the basket. "Your favorite. Sticky buns."

Grabbing a bun out of the basket, I bit into the ooey-gooey sticky goodness and chewed. It was simply orgasmic. Demi was truly one of the best pastry chefs in Manhattan.

Demi pursed her full lips. "Jesus, the vision kept looping over and over in my head. Kept me up all night. It was frustrating as hell. You know, like that annoying feeling you get when you have corn stuck in your teeth but just can't quite get the shit out?"

I nodded before rushing into the kitchen with Demi fast on my heels.

She stared at all the food. "You've been anxious-cooking again, huh?" She shoved a piece of bacon into her mouth.

"Yep," I replied before putting another piece of bun into my mouth.

"Okay... where was I?" Demi asked, tapping her chin. "Oh, yes, got it." She snapped her fingers. "And when I thought I was going to lose my fucking mind from watching the poor guy getting his ass kicked"—she jabbed a finger at me—"you popped into the vision, kneeling beside him and saving his life."

"You saw that?" I croaked, trying hard not to lose my shit. *This is bad.*

She pointed at me. "You fed him your blood. Your dad is going to kill you for breaking vampire law."

"Tell me something I don't know," I grumbled.

"Ouch! What the hell?" Jackal bellowed.

I tensed. *Damn. Shit is about to hit the fan. The wolf is on the move.*

Jackal walked into the room, looking like he could bench-press a car. His buzz-cut black hair was still damp from the shower. I wanted to glance away but was riveted to the muscles flexing across his wide chest. My eyes trailed down his belly, stopping at his jeans riding low on his hips.

"Oh God, it's him," Demi gushed, bouncing up and down like he was some damn rock star. "And he's even hotter and bigger in person." Her lips curled up while she fanned herself.

I poked her in the side. "Didn't your mama ever tell you it's rude to stare?" Then I eyeballed Jackal. "And where's your shirt, shifter?"

Jackal was insufferably annoying. One minute, I wanted to

gouge his eyes out, and the next, I wanted to lick him like a lollipop. But I drew the line at being second to any woman, and it seemed Josie was number one in his life.

He shrugged one massive shoulder. "It's ruined."

Shit. Now I had to look at Mr. Perfection strutting around my townhouse without a shirt. *This shit is getting ridiculous.*

"No worries. Reason and I are perfectly cool with eye-fucking you." Demi grinned, twirling a strand of her hair.

Jackal laughed. "That's nice to know." He arched a brow.

"I'm Demi, Reason's bestie." She dramatically fluttered her eyelashes. "And you are?"

"Jack Alagona—Jackal. Enforcer for the Alfero pack." His eyes widened at all the food piled on plates on the granite counter. He stared at me. "You cooking for an army?"

"Seems so," I muttered.

He stepped in front of me, deliberately trapping my body against the counter while reaching around me to grab a strip of bacon.

Jesus. He smelled like my body wash mixed with his cedar and sandalwood scent. Jackal was trouble with a capital T.

"Do you mind?" I pushed against his chest, but to no avail. He was built like a brick wall.

Clenching my teeth with irritation, I counted in my head, vowing to punch him in the throat if he didn't move by five. *One... two... three... three and a half...*

"Sorry," he spoke huskily. But the smirk on his face told me he was far from apologetic. Stepping back, he bit off half of the bacon strip. "Here." He handed me the rest of it.

I shook my head. "No."

He stepped forward again. With one hand, he gently grabbed my jaw, and with his other, he held the bacon to my lips. "Open up, baby. You must be starved."

Hells yes. I was hungry, ready, and willing to devour wolfie until I was satisfied.

My lips parted, and he put the bacon into my mouth. I chewed while we watched each other in some weird trance. Abruptly, he dropped his hand before storming over to my refrigerator.

Demi stared at me with wide eyes, mouthing, *That was hot.*

My traitorous lady bits must have agreed because they were damp as hell.

Damn you, pussy. Now I was more determined than ever to get Jackal the hell out of my house before I did something stupid, like dashing everything off the counter and begging him to fuck me doggy style.

I watched as he strode around my kitchen, all comfortable, like he belonged there. After taking a bottle of orange juice out of the refrigerator, he popped off the top and started to drink it straight out of the container.

"Hey, hey!" I snapped, springing into action, pushing away from the counter. "Glass, wolfie." I reached into the cabinet, pulled out a glass, and shoved it into his beefy hand.

"A little uptight, aren't you?" Jackal put the glass onto the counter before pulling out a stool tucked next to the island. He sat down and poured himself a glass of juice.

"Yeah, why don't you make yourself at home?" I spit.

Now his mere presence was irritating the hell out of me.

He eyed me while guzzling the contents of his glass. His eyes had an almost smoldering undertone. My stomach clenched. Sweat trickled between my breasts. My fingers twitched like I was a junkie craving my next fix.

I needed to keep myself from tackling him to the kitchen floor and screaming, *Touchdown!*

Pulling down an empty plate, I piled food onto it and shoved it in front of him. "Here. Eat and be gone, Jackal."

He tilted his head and studied me.

Drumming my fingers against the counter, I grumbled under my breath, "Where the fuck is Ryker?"

He watched me with those devastating green eyes, his expression giving nothing away. "Can't wait to get rid of me, huh?"

"Yes," I blurted out.

Demi watched us with wide eyes. "Well, this is fucking awkward," she mumbled before scrambling out of the kitchen and sitting down on the couch.

"Well, guess what, vampire? I'm not leaving until you tell me why and how I got here." He picked up a piece of bacon from the plate and bit off a piece. "And on that note, I need to understand what the fuck is going on with my senses."

Oh damn. Play it cool. "What about your senses?" I asked.

"I can smell the ingredients in your perfume—vanilla, jasmine, clove..." He glared at my tapping fingers. "And stop with the fucking tapping of the nails. It sounds like a jackhammer every time they hit the counter."

Instantly, my fingers froze.

He continued. "And by the way, I know whatever it is you're hiding is really bad. A trickle of sweat is running down the back of your left ear."

I reached up behind my ear, pulling away damp fingers. *What. The. Fuck?*

I glanced over at Demi, who was staring at us with rapt attention.

She mouthed, *Tell him.*

I shook my head.

Demi shrugged and continued texting on her cell.

"Eyes on me, vampire," Jackal commanded.

My head snapped back to stare at him. Jackal was glaring at me like a disapproving teacher about to bend me over his knee and slap my ass... hard.

My breaths became ragged, my nipples tightened, and warmth pooled between my thighs. *Shit, Reason, get your mind out of the damn gutter.*

He leaned forward, examining me like a specimen under a microscope. "Curious thing... All my wounds are completely healed, and that doesn't normally happen overnight, even when I shift into my wolf. So what did you do, vampire?" His jaw tensed. "I hope it wasn't something real stupid."

"Hey, guys!" Demi shouted, not even bothering to peer up from her cell. "I hate to interrupt your tense standoff, but the doorbell is about to ring."

Jackal stared at her like she had two heads.

"I'm a witch with a gift for predicting the future." She gave him a dazzling smile.

"Interesting," he replied. "What's your accuracy rate?"

"Ninety-five percent," she answered, followed by a grin.

I snorted. "More like fifty percent."

Granted, Demi was the daughter of a powerful coven high priestess with renowned psychic abilities. But due to her erratic personality and unreliable gift, her predictions almost never made sense.

Seconds later, the doorbell rang.

Demi's expression was smug. "Like I said, door, and it's the shifter's friend."

Jackal arched a brow at me.

I shrugged. "What can I say? She's having a winning streak."

I wasn't lying when I said fifty percent, but lately, her predictions had been turning out to be accurate as hell. First, she'd predicted that Light would find a cure to her empath dilemma with the Bringer of Death, which had turned out to be her new mate, Ryker; then she'd had a vision about Jackal's attack last night; and now the doorbell had rung.

I stormed over to the door and flung it open. Rip was standing there with all his blond, blue-eyed surfer-guy swagger.

I glanced over my shoulder at Jackal. "It's for you. Now grab your leash and leave my house."

"Can I come in?" Rip asked, stepping over the threshold.

"Nope." Pushing my hand against his chest, I kept him firmly in place. "Your pack mate is leaving."

"Not before we sort out this shit," Jackal barked.

Rip sidestepped me and promptly walked past me and into my house, heading right over to Demi. "Hello. My name is Rip. Enforcer for the Alfero pack. And you are?"

I slammed the door before walking over to the chaise across from Demi and sitting down.

Demi arched a brow at Rip. "Why are you talking to me?"

"Because you're sitting here in all your beautiful glory."

He gave her a thousand-watt smile I was sure melted hundreds of panties off susceptible women, but it wasn't working on Demi. In fact, she looked like she was seconds away from Superman-punching him in the face.

Demi peered at me. "Again... why is he talking to me? I don't converse with idiots."

Jackal walked over to the couch and sat down next to Demi with arms crossed, intently staring at me.

"Do you two know each other?" I asked.

In unison, Demi shouted, "Yes!" while Rip drawled, "No."

"Which is it?" Jackal asked.

"Well, I had two visions with him in it," Demi replied.

"She's a psychic witch," I directed to Rip.

Demi pointed at Rip. "In one of my visions, the blond Adonis and I were having freaky, naughty sex."

Rip wiggled his eyebrows. "Sounds promising, darling."

Demi rolled her eyes. "And in the other, I caught him cheating on me with some big-breasted brunette in his bed." Demi stood up and poked him in the chest hard before walking away, mumbling about, "Wolf-shifters who can't keep their big cocks in their pants." She sat down next to me.

Rip frowned. "Well, that's new. I'm not used to the ladies running away from me."

"Get used to it, shifter," Demi advised.

Damn. I felt a major migraine developing. This was way too much drama for me to stomach first thing in the morning. I was accustomed to peace and quiet. But with Jackal invading my space and the dynamic duo, Rip and Demi, I was close to going batshit crazy on all their asses.

Rip frowned. "Jackal, let's go home. I have better things to do today."

"Wait, you two live together?" Demi's eyes widened with fake innocence. "Are you lovers?" she asked with a snide expression on her face.

Jackal snorted. "What the hell are you talking about, witch? I'm not fucking him. We live at Ryker's compound. In separate apartments."

"Yeah... right," Demi replied.

"I'd be happy to prove how much I love women, darling." Rip regarded Demi with sexual interest written all over his face.

Demi rolled her eyes. "Shifter, don't hold your breath. You and I are not copulating."

His eyes narrowed. "I have no clue what you're talking about, beautiful."

Demi sighed before glancing over at me. "He's not too smart, is he?" She stared over at him. "*Copulate*, as in *to fuck*," she uttered with evident sarcasm.

Rip cut in. "I know what the hell *copulate* means, darling, but I've just never heard anyone use the word in casual conversation in quite the way you just did."

She pointed at him. "Don't talk anymore."

He growled, "Okay, I'm out. I don't need this shit."

"I'm not going anywhere," Jackal insisted, "not until Reason tells me how I ended up here." He frowned. "The last thing I remember is giving the Shadows a good fight."

I snorted. "You call that a good fight? They stabbed you multiple times and tried to break every bone in your body. You were almost dead before I arrived and saved your life."

His hands flew up to his neck with fingers probing around.

"No, I did not bite you, wolfie," I informed.

He stood up, marching over to me. "Then what did you do to me, vampire?"

My pulse accelerated at his question. "I gave you my blood," I responded quietly, not the least bit intimidated by the fact that he was towering over me, pissed as hell. Shit, in truth, his anger turned me on—big time. *God, I'm so fucked up in the head.*

He pinned me under a hard stare. "You turned me into a damn vampire?"

My irritation swelled. "Of course not, idiot. To turn you, I would have to bite you, infecting you with my saliva." I impatiently waved my hand. "Why am I even explaining this to you? The point is I brought you back from the edge of death by giving you my blood." I paused, mulling over the new clusterfuck. Me giving him my blood seemed to have heightened all his shifter senses. "So stand down, doggy, and just say thank you to the nice vampire."

"You want me to say thank you for fucking up my life?"

I jumped up, jamming my hands onto my hips. "Yes. You should be grateful, shifter."

"Grateful?" he bellowed. "Woman, you sound deranged." He paused. "Are my heightened senses temporary or permanent?"

I blinked rapidly. "Don't know." I didn't.

"You don't know?" He ran a hand across his hair. "You can't just make life-altering decisions without doing some analysis beforehand." He paced back and forth.

The calculating, logical lawyer in me knew he was right, but something in me had snapped last night when I saw him near death. Anyone else, I would have walked away, but not Jackal. Something inside me had compelled me to save him, despite the consequences of my possible death. Anger stirred deep in my gut. He had no damn clue of the sacrifice I'd made for his ass.

What an ungrateful fucker.

"Would you rather be dead?" I almost held my breath, waiting for his answer.

He stopped in his tracks. Tone as flat as ever, he replied, "Yes. I don't want filthy vampire blood in my body."

I flinched as if he'd psychically slapped me. *Filthy vampire blood? Is that what he thinks about me?*

Normally, my thick skin would have sloughed his words off, but surprisingly, they'd pierced my armor, hurting me to the damn core.

"Oh, fuck no, shifter!" Demi yelled. "You don't talk to her like that."

I raised my hand. "I got this, Demi."

Storming over to him, I shoved him hard. He didn't budge.

"You fucking bastard," I bit the words out. "I saved your life, and you insult me?"

He grabbed my hands, pulling me against his chest. "I didn't mean it. The words—"

My breath caught in my throat as I blinked hard. "Let me go," I muttered.

"Reason." His nostrils flared.

"Now." My lips flattened.

He released me with his lips pressed in a slight grimace.

I eyed him with my chin high. "And now that we are being so open and honest about this shit, I don't think you'll be able to shift. Your wolf is injured or something."

"How would you know that?" Jackal's fists clenched and unclenched.

"I don't know, but I do."

There was tightness in his eyes. "But if you can sense my wolf, maybe you can reverse what you did."

I finally threw my arms up in the air with exasperation. "I can't coax it out of its shell like it's some fucking turtle, Jackal."

"This is bullshit," he roared. "You fucked up my senses and my wolf."

His tone ignited my temper. I was seriously contemplating punching him in the throat.

"You damn unappreciative bastard. I broke vampire law by giving you my blood. If anyone finds out, I'll be facing death."

"I don't give a shit. I didn't ask for this," Jackal finished while dashing things off my credenza.

I flinched. "You just broke my damn vase!" I shrieked. "You owe me twenty-five hundred dollars."

He pushed off another one. "Add that to my bill, vampire."

"You fucker!" I delivered between clenched teeth.

Demi stood up. "Okay, both of you, stop." She glared at Jackal. "All she knows is that your wolf is injured, and she's speculating it might have something to do with the blood she fed you." She glanced at me. "Right?"

"Right," I confirmed.

Jackal growled, "How could you have made such a big mistake like that?"

"Asshole, didn't I just explain I've never given someone blood before?" I incredulously looked around.

"Reason, you're not helping," Demi declared.

I held up my hands. "Okay, I'll be nice and patient with the dumbass shifter." I paused. "I spent years studying the process of vampires feeding their blood to others. I swear I didn't do anything wrong."

"I think you need to do a lot more studying, darling," Jackal spoke sharply.

"You're fucking rude." I bit the words out.

"I'm entitled, don't you think?" he retorted.

I jabbed my finger in his face. "You ought to be grateful I saved your ass, wolfie, because you were almost dead."

"If I'm not a shifter, then what the fuck am I? Some sort of hybrid like you? No fucking thanks, vampire. Like I said, I'd rather be fucking dead."

"Okay, I'm so done with this fucking conversation." I stormed over to the door, flinging it open. "This is your cue, wolfie. Grab your leash and get the fuck out. Now."

Rip shook his head. "Come on, Jackal. This is going nowhere." He walked out of my house without another word.

"Fine," Jackal grumbled, charging over to the open door. "This is far from over, Reason."

"As far as I'm concerned, it is." I gestured for him to get the hell out.

He snarled before stepping through the threshold.

I slammed the door behind him. "Good riddance."

❧ 7 ❧

REASON

WHEN I ENTERED MY OFFICE, my eyes darted toward the mahogany desk and the two mountains of paper piled neatly on it. Client files and unopened mail. Well, at least Tabitha had attempted to organize the chaos before she left today.

"Just another fucking day in Orlov paradise," I declared before dropping my designer handbag on my leather sofa on the way to my desk. Pulling out the plush leather chair, I plopped down with a loud, tired sigh. I needed a long vacation somewhere hot, sunny, sandy, and without an Other in sight.

But I'd be damned if I admitted to my workaholic dad that I was exhausted. I was becoming a walking zombie from too much work and not enough sleep. My mind and body were heading for a painful crash. But I was determined to push on.

"Shit. Why the hell did Tabitha have to go on vacation with that bear-shifter?" I complained with a tinge of jealousy burning in me before quickly dashing it away.

I was happy that she'd finally found her mate, which was like finding a needle in a haystack. My eyebrows furrowed. Lately, it'd seemed like a lot of my friends were finding love and their mates. First, it was Storm, then Light, and now Tabitha. *It must be something in the fucking drinking water.*

Note to self: stick with bottled water indefinitely.

Quickly, I started mentally cataloguing all the things that needed to be done immediately. Hiring another attorney to help with our clients was at the top of the list. But the ideal candidate would need to have one unique skill—the ability to adapt to Dad's abrupt and demanding personality. He was an absolute nightmare to work with and ridiculously nitpicky.

My eyes narrowed on the client files. I felt a migraine developing from just thinking about the argument that would ensue over our need to hire additional staff. Shit, I was his daughter, and he hadn't been enthusiastic about bringing me into the firm years ago. He'd thought I would be better off concentrating on finding a worthy pure-blooded vampire to settle down with.

My jaw tightened at the inevitability of my destiny now that I'd made a deal to marry Stefan. And if Ryker and his pack didn't find Light fast, I'd be married to Stefan in thirty days. As soon as I said *I do*, Dad would start putting the full-court press on me to pop out a shitload of vampire babies.

Children with Stefan? That shit is not happening. Well, not without me kicking and screaming in protest.

This was my life, and I'd be damned if I allowed Dad's or the Orlov coven's expectations of me determine the rest of my life. My work was everything to me. I'd busted my ass to prove I not only deserved to be a part of his firm, but that I was also partner material. My sacrifice was working long hours with no vacations, no social life, and no romantic relationships.

Grabbing the stack of mail, I started shuffling through it. "Junk… junk… more junk," I mumbled.

Then something in the stack of mail caught my attention. I plucked out the magazine, and my stomach plummeted when I saw the beautiful couple on the front cover of the *Others Gazette* —otherwise known as the Other society's gossip rag.

I blinked, hoping it was some sort of fucking mirage. But there he was, Charles Bailey—wolf-shifter, attorney tycoon, and my former boyfriend—on the cover with wolf-shifter Jessica Jones, the perfectly coiffed blond Hollywood celebrity attorney.

I bit my bottom lip, remembering the night I'd broken up with him.

Charles and I were at my favorite French restaurant, celebrating the first case I'd won.

He reached over, caressing my fingers. "Congrats to the smartest, sexiest vampire in Manhattan."

"Keep flattering me, shifter," I purred between sips of wine, "and we'll be skipping dessert and heading to your car for some smoking-hot foreplay."

"Check, please." He winked at me while swirling the wine in his glass. "By the way, have you thought about what we talked about last night?"

"Yes, I have." I shifted in my chair. "But there's no way my father would ever be interested in expanding the Orlov brand to California. Starting a new law firm on the West Coast is not on his agenda." Especially if it involved making Charles a partner in such an endeavor.

Dad hated Charles. In his eyes, dating a wolf-shifter was the ultimate vampire taboo. It was rare that vampires dated anyone but their own kind, but I was different and wanted more from a man. I had dated enough vampires to know they couldn't give me what I needed in a relationship. Vampires were cold and lacked the ability for affection, and unions were more for strategic power moves to further their status in vampire society.

Dad just didn't get that interspecies dating among Others was finally taking hold. It wasn't the norm, but I didn't give a shit. Charles was the man I was willing to go against Dad and the coven for. And even though it had been hell at work when my dad realized Charles and I were getting serious, nothing could kill my joy because Charles Bailey was the one I'd been waiting for all my life. He was ambitious, smart, handsome, and career-oriented. He didn't give a shit that I was the daughter of the most powerful vampire in the Northeast or that I was the coven's princess. He loved me for me. And I was willing to fight for our relationship.

Shifter or vampire, we could make this relationship work.

"Reason, this is not about him. It's about you. You don't need his approval. You have the Orlov name." He charmingly smiled at me. "What about your dreams of being free to run your life as you deem fit? Just imagine striking it out on your own with me by your side. We'd be Hollywood's top celebrity attorneys—The Orlov and Bailey Firm. How does that sound?"

"Horrible." I scrunched up my nose. "Besides, I love it in New York. I don't want to move to California."

I'd built a reputation of being thorough, cutthroat, and vicious as an attorney. Dad had finally trusted me enough to hand over one of his longest and influential clients—the Credence family. On top of that, I had been bringing in new, younger, and powerful Other clients every month, building the Orlov firm even more. I was one step closer to being made partner.

I stared at Charles and all his blond, golden perfection.

What we had wasn't love... yet. So was being with him enough to walk away from everything I'd built?

My stomach quivered. Frankly, I wasn't a hundred percent sure.

Charles laced his fingers with mine. "With me by your side, everything and anything is possible. We'd build on what we have and make it strong. Together. Forever."

Forever? Was he going to propose to me tonight? Oh God... I wasn't ready for that shit. Or was I?

"Forever? Are you actually going to put a big diamond ring on it?" I dramatically wiggled my left hand. "My dad is already foaming at the mouth about us dating." I smirked. "If we got married and had a shitload of babies, that shit would send my dad crazy."

Even though I was unapologetically dedicated to my career, my stomach fluttered with excitement at the thought of marriage, love, stability, and babies. Then I sobered up when I realized it was the notion of the white picket fence that made me giddy and not so much the man, Charles.

He quickly released my hand. "Marriage and babies? We've just started out in our careers."

I blinked in confusion.

"I'm not interested in getting married or having babies with..." He grabbed his glass and guzzled the contents.

Oh, hell no! My stomach dropped. "Finish your statement, Charles."

Had Dad been right all along about vampires and shifters not mixing?

Or worse, was he right about Charles being a pretentious, social-climbing prick?

Charles huffed before saying, "Dating you is one thing, but marriage? That's not even a remote possibility."

My back stiffened. "So you can fuck me, you can become business part-ners with me, but I'm not good enough for you to marry?" I went from sad and hurt to fucking pissed in zero seconds. I took a slow sip of water to calm my nerves as I absorbed what the motherfucker was saying to me.

I wasn't marriage material? Bullshit.

He sputtered, "Let's not trivialize this."

I slammed my glass onto the table. "Say it," I demanded through gritted teeth.

"Come on, Reason. Don't be this way."

He reached across the table to grab my hand. I pulled it out of reach.

"I love being with you, and the sex is phenomenal. You're smart and ambitious, and most importantly, you get that my career is my top priority right now."

"I need to hear you say it aloud, you damn coward." The sadistic streak in me egged me on even though I knew the words would lance my heart.

"Say what?" he barked.

"That you would never get married to me because I'm a vampire," I uttered frostily.

"Reason," he whined, "don't be difficult."

"Charles," I mocked, "just be brutally honest with me. I'm a big girl. I can take it."

"Fine. I can't marry you because you're a vampire."

My heart iced over. "Thank you. That's exactly what I needed to hear. You and I are over." I pushed back from the table and walked away without turning back.

MY THOUGHTS SNAPPED BACK TO THE PRESENT, AND MY fingers shook as I read the magazine's headline aloud, "'Hollywood's Top Attorney Finds Love at Last.' At last? What the hell was I? A fucking pit stop?" My anger rose from just thinking about the many times he had been cock deep in me, singing he *loved* me at the top of his lungs. Then the hurt settled in when I caught one little detail on the cover. Jessica was pregnant.

"Fuck him. And fuck love." I tossed the magazine into the trash can.

My office phone rang, and I automatically pressed the button on the console, activating the hands-free speaker.

"The Orlov firm," I answered while continuing my sorting.

"Hello, Miss Orlov," the male voice greeted. "It's Sam from the security desk. You have a visitor downstairs to see you. Mr. Jack Alagona. Shall I send him up?"

I sat straight up in my chair. He was the last man I wanted to see, but this was my damn office, and I wasn't about to cower or hide.

"Send him up," I ordered.

It didn't take long for me to hear the elevator door slide open, followed by the sound of heels tapping against the marble floor. Shortly thereafter, my kryptonite, Jackal, appeared in my doorway, looking like hot sex on a stick.

"Hello, Reason," he greeted with pensive eyes.

Clasping my hands in front of me, I didn't respond. I had no damn intention of making this visit easy on him.

"The silent treatment. I guess I deserve that." He prowled closer with his gaze pinning me to the spot.

"What do you want, Jackal?" I despised the huskiness of my

voice and the way my stomach flip-flopped with excitement from his mere presence.

He smiled in his bad-boy sort of way and then started to sit down in the chair in front of my desk.

I stopped him with a curt, "Don't you dare sit your ass down. You're not going to be here long."

He sat down anyway. "It's like that, huh?" His eyes bored into me.

I arched a well-manicured brow. "Why are you here?"

"I'm taking you out for dinner."

My mouth flopped open and then closed. "So you presume that, one, I'm available and, two, I really give a shit what you want?"

I had to hand it to him; he was one ballsy shifter.

His green eyes darkened like clouds before an impending storm. "You're not available?"

I watched him like he had two heads. "I am not. Now, if that's all—" My cell rang. I glanced around for my handbag and found it lying on the sofa where I'd left it. Quickly standing up, I walked over, pulled it out of my bag, and immediately recognized the number.

"Yes, Stefan?" I answered, storming over to my desk and perching myself at the edge.

"You're just rainbows and sunshine, aren't you?" Jackal grumbled.

I ignored him.

"Where are you?" Stefan demanded. "I just dropped by your place, and you're not there."

I was exhausted from Stefan's misplaced possessiveness. Jesus, between Jackal and Stefan, I was one step away from going Brooklyn crazy on these domineering alpha assholes.

"And?" I snapped.

I blinked in confusion when I felt Jackal's fingers caressing my outer thigh.

Stop it, I mouthed.

What? he mouthed back while watching me like a mischievous bad boy.

"You know the deal, Reason," Stefan snapped. "You call and check in with me so I can inform your father that you're safe. That's not negotiable. Do you want me to slap a full twenty-four-seven detail on your ass, starting tonight?"

His statement set my teeth on edge. Stefan was overstepping his authority again and, to boot, pissing me the fuck off.

"First, you don't have the balls or authority to do that, Stefan. And second, don't make me flex my bitch power and have you killed for talking to me in such a high-handed manner." I swiped my finger over my cell's screen, ending the call.

It never failed. Stefan knew exactly what buttons to push to rile me up. He knew how much I hated the security detail Dad had assigned to me since I was old enough to walk. Those men allotted me no privacy and were quick to snitch on my every move to Dad, like good little enforcers. And one day, I'd just said enough was enough, giving Dad an ultimatum. He either removed my detail, or I'd disappear from New York and never come back. It wasn't a bluff; I'd meant it.

In typical lawyer fashion, we'd brokered a deal. I'd promised I'd check in with him several times a day, and he'd remove the security watch. Easy. But when Stefan had stepped into Dimitri's position as head enforcer, he'd started acting like the new sheriff in town and begun randomly stopping by my townhouse to check on me.

"You and that prick Stefan dating?" Jackal's velvet rasp was nearing a guttural growl.

"That would be none of your damn business," I replied. "And why are you still here, Jackal?" I was losing patience with him and wanted him gone.

In the blink of an eye, Jackal was looming over me, crowding my space. "Like I said, I'm taking you to dinner," he grated.

My first instinct was to move, but I knew shifters; any

attempt to evade him would kick in his wolf instinct to chase. "Not interested. Next."

His eyes narrowed. "I also want to apologize for what I said to you this morning."

"For which part? The verbal slap for saving your ass with my blood? Or when you made me feel like shit for being part vampire?"

"Both," he grunted.

"Both, huh? How noble of you." I pursed my lips.

"Cut me some slack, Reason." He crossed his beefy arms. "I was fucking upset about being fed vampire blood." He blew out a breath. "I was wrong to talk to you the way I did. I apologize for being an asshole. But hearing what you did, combined with coming to terms with something being wrong with my wolf... well, it really threw me for a loop."

I wasn't insensitive to the quagmire I'd created by feeding him my blood, but I also wasn't going to be shamed for making the life-or-death decision.

"So I should have let you die?" I asked.

"Yes," he snapped. "Without my ability to shift, I'm lost." He ran his fingers across his buzz-cut hair. "You're a vampire, so you wouldn't understand what that means to a shifter."

I threw my hands in the air with exasperation. "Oh, for fuck's sake. Let's cut to the damn chase, shall we? What's your problem with me?"

He growled, scrubbing his fingers against his face, before replying, "Vampires and shifters don't mix. You know this."

I eyed him coldly. "Let me get this straight. You don't like me because of some antiquated, centuries-old prejudice and propaganda about vampires?" My fists curled and disappointment burned in the pit of my stomach. "You don't know how bad I want to Superman-punch you in the face right now." I didn't need this shit. "You know what?" I pointed to the door. "Get the fuck out of my office. I'm done with this conversation."

"I'm not leaving until I say my piece." Jackal leaned forward, reaching down to cup the back of my head. "I like you, Reason, probably more than I should. But I can't give you what you deserve from a man. I'm broken. I'm no good for any woman." His voice cracked.

The despair and sadness that laced his voice nearly broke me a little inside. My mind flicked over to the woman's name he'd whispered in my bed.

Damn, what did this Josie woman do to the man?

I arched a brow. "So now you think you know what I want?"

"What I'm—"

"Okay, enough." I cut him off. "I have to say this." I swallowed over my nervousness because, frankly, I wasn't the most eloquent in relaying my feelings. "When I saw you dying and bloody in that alley, I felt something. A magnetic pull I've never felt with any man." I cupped his chiseled, lightly stubbled cheek. "And honestly, it's fucking scary... this strange, weird connection between us that I don't really understand. And the crazy thing is I'm willing to explore where it would take me... us. But I will not beg you to take this journey with me." My hand dropped away.

He pressed his forehead against mine while releasing his grip on my hair. "I can't, Reason."

I leaned away from him. "You mean you won't." I took a deep breath, pushing down the sadness that tightened my chest. "So it's not about you or me from this point onward. It's about our mutual interest—finding where the Shadows are holding Light. On that note, you can tell Ryker I've convinced my father to help him get her back. Once that's done, you and I will have nothing more to say to each other."

"You convinced your father to help get Light back? How?"

"Get your nose out of my business." Pressing my palm flat against his chest, pushing slightly, I ordered, "Step aside. This meeting is adjourned, shifter."

He didn't resist moving back, allowing me to brush past him and take a seat behind my desk. I felt his hot, scorching stare but didn't cave in to my heart's desire to meet his eyes. Pulling the stack of folders closest to me, I refused to peer up until I heard his retreating steps, followed by the opening and closing of the elevator door.

My head snapped up, and I stared into space, hating myself for wanting a man who didn't want me.

~

Normally, working late into the night was cathartic and cleared my head, but not tonight. Trying to work the memory of Jackal away had just made me even sadder.

Stepping out of my office elevator, I landed in the well-lit, deserted underground parking lot. The only things I looked forward to were a long, hot, fragrant bath with lavender salts and a large glass—maybe two—of wine to drown my sorrows.

My feet faltered when I spotted Jackal leaning against a sleek black Porsche, arms crossed against his massive chest.

I glided past him toward my luxury vehicle parked beside his. "What are you still doing here?" I asked, pressing my key fob, automatically unlocking my automobile. "Don't you have anything else to do besides stalk me?"

"Do you always work this late?" he grated.

Not bothering to gaze at him, I answered, "Yes, I do. Not that it's any of your damn business." I yanked open my driver's door, tossing my handbag onto the passenger seat. "Now skedaddle. I have shit to do." *And a bottle of expensive wine to guzzle.*

I yelped when I felt his arm wrap around my waist, yanking me flush against his body. The heat of his chest muscles radiated against my back. *Damn the shifter's wily ways.*

"I'm not leaving until you agree to let me take you out to dinner," he growled against my ear.

It sent an involuntary shiver of want down my spine, but I refused to fold like a deck of cards.

"I'm not interested." My fingernails dug into his forearm,

attempting to pry him away from me... but to no avail. "And what's with the touching?"

"I happen to love touching you, vampire."

I stilled. "I'm not doing this, Jackal."

He unwrapped his arm from my waist, twisting me around to face him. "Doing what?" he asked, caging me with his delicious body.

"This." I gestured to his body pressed against mine. "One minute, you're pushing me away. The next, you're all over me. Frankly, I don't have the time or patience to play Jedi mind games."

"It's not like that. It's not you," he spoke in his quiet, rough voice. "It's me."

I quirked a brow in his direction. "Are you really giving me the it's-not-you-it's-me speech?"

"It's complicated. Just give me the opportunity to explain myself over dinner."

"I'm not hungry." My stomach growled loudly, contradicting me. *Dammit!*

"You sound hungry." He tilted his head and studied me.

I sighed, giving up the pretense of neutrality to Jackal's charm. "Dinner. That's all."

"You won't regret it. I promise you." Jackal grinned. "Let's take my car."

He clasped my fingers, ushering me over to his vehicle. After he opened the door for me, I slid into his car, sinking into the plush leather and watching Jackal's magnificent ass as he strode around to hop into the driver's seat.

Shit, this is a big damn mistake. Why am I such a glutton for punishment?

❧ 8 ❧

JACKAL

Swerving through Manhattan traffic, I easily spotted the vehicle trailing me. Just as we—Ryker, Soar, Rip, and I—had planned, the Shadows had taken the bait. I sped up a little just to toy with the driver, but I was careful to ensure the car wouldn't lose me. The tailing automobile weaved in and out of traffic, cutting off several yellow cabs.

Fucking amateur.

I slowed down. Game time was over. I needed the Shadows for the plan we'd carefully concocted to work. Stopping at the red light, I glanced over at Reason, who was sitting in the passenger seat, staring out the window. Despite the fact that we hadn't uttered a word since we left her law firm's underground parking garage, the silence between us was strangely comfortable.

She turned to examine me, as if she'd felt my stare. "So where are we heading to for dinner?"

"Redemption."

I wasn't enthusiastic about patronizing the place, but I had to stick to the plan. Reason and I had to be seen publicly together in a location that was highly frequented by Others, and Redemption was the only logical choice.

"You want to go back there after the wicked beatdown you just took?" Her lips twisted into a smirk.

"I was outnumbered," I grumbled. "That shit wouldn't have gone down if it had been a one-on-one fight."

"Uh-huh." She rolled her eyes. "How about we try something different? I've heard a lot of buzz about this new place called Angels."

"Hard pass on Angels." My eyes narrowed. "It's not your speed."

"Excuse me? What makes you think it's not my speed?" She blinked a couple times. "Wait, have you been there before?"

I cleared my throat. "Several times," I mumbled, leaving out the fact that *several times* meant every Friday and Saturday night since the fucking place had opened three months ago. "It's an Others-only establishment."

"Sounds perfect," she chirped.

Only if you like your dinner and drinks served with a sideshow of ass and tits.

I blew out a breath of frustration. "Okay, here's the deal. Angels is mainly frequented by men because of the eye-candy Nephilim who work both floors. The lounge upstairs and the restaurant downstairs."

She burst out laughing. "Shit. I'm learning all sorts of wonderful things about you this week, shifter. You have a freaky, naughty Nephilim fetish, and you can't fight to save your damn life. And just so we're clear, we're going to Angels because I've heard the food is excellent, and it's the only place you probably won't run the risk of getting your ass kicked again."

"If you mention that Shadows shit again, I swear I'll pull over, put you over my lap, and slap your sweet ass until you beg me to stop."

"Oh, goody." She clapped her hands and playfully bounced up and down. "Promise?"

My inner beast snarled and viciously clawed my insides.

Ouch, you fucker. What was that for? I mentally snarled at my wolf.

My wolf grouched back, *She thinks we can't protect her. Show her we can. Shift. Now.*

I growled menacingly, showing my beast my dominance before answering with, *Okay... no more. You're on a time-out.* Then I securely caged him for the duration of the night.

Not that I blamed my wolf for his attraction to Reason. Within the confines of my vehicle, her sweet jasmine, vanilla, and clove scent was deliciously intoxicating. *Damn vampire.* My cock stirred and stiffened, straining against my pants.

My cell rang, and I sighed with relief. I needed a distraction before I pulled over into some secluded area and begged Reason for the privilege of fucking her senseless.

Tapping my earpiece, I answered, "What's up?"

"Is the plan in play?" Soar countered.

"Yes," I replied shortly, not wanting to reveal too much to Reason.

"Good. I'll let Ryker know. He was concerned about the Shadows not taking the lure. We need them to follow you for our strategy to succeed."

"Got it. I'm on my way to Angels with Reason," I replied impatiently. "I'll catch you later."

"Wait, don't hang up," he demanded sharply. "There's something you need to know. Our servers were hacked and data was stolen."

My back stiffened. "Shit," I mumbled under my breath. "Did they access our video surveillance system?"

"Don't know yet. I'm working on determining who hacked us and what data was compromised."

"Okay. As soon as you complete your analysis, call me ASAP. I need to know if they got into the Redemption surveillance footage." Ending our call, I pulled out my earpiece.

God, I hoped they hadn't gotten the footage taken the night the Shadows attacked me. If that evidence got in the wrong hands, the fallout from what Reason had done to save my life would destroy hers.

"What Redemption surveillance?" Reason inquired.

I struggled with exactly how much I should tell her. Not that I didn't trust her. I didn't trust what her father would do if he knew one of the first things Ryker had done when he took over as leader of the Other Council was start secret video surveillance on Redemption. Ryker wanted to keep tabs on Oskar, who frequented the establishment.

"Come on, Jackal." She placed a hand on my thigh. "You can trust me."

I sighed heavily. "We have twenty-four-seven video surveillance on Redemption."

"To spy on my father," she astutely guessed.

"How did you know?"

She shrugged. "He has surveillance on your pack. So I naturally assumed you'd return the favor. But what I find ironic is that so much time and effort was put into keeping tabs on each other that no one saw the real threat. The Shadows." She shook her head. "Shifters and vampires need to get their shit together and put their petty animosity aside. If they don't, they'll never win this war against the Shadows."

She was right. The Shadows were exploiting the hate and distrust we had for each other and strategically using it to divide and conquer.

"I agree." I pulled off at the green light. My eyes flitted to the rearview mirror. The black car was still following us. With eyes firmly on the road, I weaved into the late-night Manhattan congestion. "That's why your father pulling out of the negotiation for a permanent peace pact has hurt Ryker's cause to unite the Others."

"I can't dispute your point, Jackal. But as much as I would like my dad to move forward with the negotiation, he won't. On a positive note, he is sympathetic to Ryker's plight with finding

Light and has sworn to me that he will offer his top enforcers and resources to help you guys out."

Did she say her father was sympathetic? I bit back a snort.

She was fucking delusional. Her father was a manipulative fucker who didn't give a shit about anyone but himself.

"Bullshit. What's in it for him?"

"None of your concern, Jackal," she snapped, snatching her hand away from my leg.

"You're testing my patience, darling."

"Like I give a shit, wolfie."

I growled with impatience.

She mocked me by growling back. "This is fun—ruffling your fur."

I moved my hand to her thigh. "If you want fun"—pressing my fingers into the fabric of her dress, I raked them up her leg, and Reason gasped—"I have way more exciting and sweaty things we can do, vampire."

She shoved my hand away. "Oh, stop being a cunt-tease." Her voice was husky before she cleared her throat. "Back to my dad and his willingness to help Ryker. Let's just say my father and I have come to an agreement. And before you ask, the terms are personal."

I wanted to delve further into exactly what these terms were, but Reason was a stubborn woman. She wouldn't reveal anything unless she damn well wanted to.

My eyebrows furrowed. But the bigger issue was that her sneaky father had been making lots of secret agreements lately—with Ryker and the Shadows and now with her.

What is the vampire fucker up to? Is he playing all of us against each other?

My hand tightened around the steering wheel. I had told Ryker I didn't trust Orlov and that we didn't need him to help us get Light back. But the rest of the pack had overruled me. We'd made a pact with the devil—Oskar Orlov. I just hoped it wouldn't come back to bite us on the ass.

"Shit. Wait a damn minute," Reason hissed. "If there's video surveillance on Redemption, then that means I was being recorded when I gave you blood."

I cleared my throat. "Kind of." I approached Angels, parking in plain sight but far enough away from the establishment to allow the trailing vehicle to park without detection.

She glared at me with wild eyes. "What do you mean kind of?"

Turning off my vehicle, I stared at her.

"Well, shifter?" She unbuckled her seat belt, turning her body completely and pinning me in place with her don't-fuck-with-me stare. "It's either yes or no. And don't you dare lie to me."

"First, I would never lie to you, Reason. Second, yes, that night was recorded, but we're not sure they accessed—"

She held up her hand, cutting me off. "Accessed? You were hacked?"

"Yes."

Her eyes widened. "Who? What? Oh God... if my father finds out what I did... I'm dead. Literally."

"Let's not jump to any conclusions. We don't know if they hacked our surveillance system. So there's no need to panic until we know for sure." I cupped her cheek. "Darling, just breathe and relax until we know more. There's really nothing we can do."

Reason took a calming deep breath. "The minute you know..."

"I'll call you. I promise. And if the data from the night was compromised, you and I will figure out how to handle the fallout... together." I kissed her on the lips before pulling back. "Now let's not ruin a good night. Dinner, drinks, and hopefully lots of bad decisions are in store." I wiggled my eyebrows.

She laughed before giving me a mock stern stare. "Let's get this circus over with."

I hopped out, making my way to open the door for Reason.

She stepped out onto the sidewalk and then froze. "Something feels"—her eyes panned the streets—"wrong."

Damn. Did she sense the Shadows lurking?

We'd worked on a strategy that just might tip the scale in our favor. It was our Hail Mary because, at this point, we didn't have anything else. Not that I was completely comfortable with this plan, but we had no other options. We had to get Light from the Shadows's clutches. The upside was we knew Light wasn't dead because Ryker could sense her through their mate bond. The downside was the link was getting weaker every day.

"It's probably nothing," I replied, infusing a hint of nonchalance in my tone. "Besides, if anyone tries anything, I'll hand out a beatdown." I winked at her.

"Yeah, sure." She smirked. "I've seen your fighting skills."

"Come on, smartass," I said with a light touch on her elbow.

I ushered her along SoHo's picturesque cobblestone streets and past cast-iron buildings before steering her down a wide alleyway.

"Jesus, it's creepy and dark here." Reason blew out her breath as the alleyway became so narrow we had to walk single file. "Why would anyone put a restaurant in this location?"

"It's discreet and deters humans from venturing down here."

"Shit, I can't disagree with you there," she muttered before we finally stood in front of a nondescript black door with a dusty keypad attached. "What now?"

I punched in the code that all regulars and invited guests were given. The lock clicked, and the door slid open, revealing the dimly lit interior of the large renovated manufacturing building. The inconspicuous doorman closed the door behind us with a slight nod.

Always vigilant, I scanned the area and filtered through the numerous cloying scents—shifters, witches, vampires, and angels —that lingered in the air. Satisfied there were no imminent threats inside, I allowed myself to relax a little. With a long waiting list, Angels was the place to see and be seen. It was more of a VIP restaurant and lounge, patronized by Others who loved the mystique of hybrid angels. It was also known that Kellita, a

Nephilim—hybrid angel and human—and the owner of the establishment, scrutinized each guest.

Gently nudging Reason in front of me, I wondered what she thought about the sexy decor—all red velvet, black chandeliers, dim lights, and heavy velvet curtains. But I didn't utter a word as she glided through the throng of customers waiting to be seated with a sensual sway that made both men and women stare.

Shit, I didn't blame them. Reason was luminous with her perfect smile and smooth brown skin. Her body-hugging black dress slid over her curves like it had been designed solely for her. Its hemline stopped several inches above her knees, allowing me a glimpse of skin.

She was part smolder and part fury as she walked through the patrons.

Tall and curvy, she made my fingers clench. I unabashedly craved her. From the moment she'd sat down in my car, I'd been fighting to keep my mind off her intoxicating scent, but her honey-sweet aroma had filled the air like perfume. My wolf had rattled his cage, fighting to get out. My hands had clutched the steering wheel as I tried to contain my inner beast with all my might.

My loins twitched from just thinking about all the dirty, filthy, sensual ways I could destroy her sinful body—her on all fours with my one hand gripping her full ass and the other wrapped around the strands of her hair while I fucked her from behind.

Easy, man. She doesn't belong to you.

My inner wolf thought otherwise. *She's mine,* he growled in my head. *Mark her. Now,* he finished with a huff.

She's not yours. She's ours, I hissed back at him.

Finally... we agree, my beast replied smugly.

Shit... the fucker tricked me into verbalizing what I have on countless occasions denied.

Kellita—a voluptuous brunette wearing skintight leather leggings and a red corset that pushed up her ample cleavage—

approached us with a huge smile. "Sweet baby Jesus. Jackal, you brought a date to my humble establishment? Wow. This is a fucking first." Kellita's gaze fell on Reason. "Oh, honey, you're way too pretty and classy for this guy."

Reason boldly stared back at her. "A woman who recognizes greatness," she replied cheekily. "I like you already."

Kellita clapped her hands together with glee. "Oh, Jackal, this one is a spitfire. She won't be putting up with any of your bullshit."

"Not at all," Reason interjected.

I shot Reason a warning glare, but she just laughed.

Kellita gave Reason a mock stern stare. "Just so you know, he's a manwhore who has been spoiled by all the wrong women. So it's going to take a lot of work to whip his ass into shape."

Kellita winked at me. I frowned at her quip.

"Okay, let's find you the best table in the house," she chirped before snapping her fingers. "Lucky!"

A monstrous man swooped out of nowhere, looking like a reject Thor impersonator, except with red hair. "Yes?" he asked with a thick Irish accent, his eyes glued on Reason like she was a tasty steak he wanted to gobble up.

Reason craned her head all the way back to stare at Lucky.

Oh, fuck no. I stepped forward to stake my claim on Reason.

Kellita grabbed my forearm. "Bad shifter," she reprimanded. "Lucky, will you please escort our lovely guest to our best table," she purred. "I need a minute with Jackal."

"My pleasure," the red-haired prick growled. Then the show-off flexed his muscles before his big white wings morphed out of his back, flicking out wide, as if he were about to take flight.

Reason clapped loudly. "Wow. It's Lucky the angel, and he's magically delicious." Her lips curled up into a wide smile with eyes gleaming like a kid in a candy shop. "I can't wait to come here again with my besties, Demi, Storm, and Light."

"Sweetheart, the more the merrier." Lucky shook his feathers, and one of his disgusting angelic wings almost slapped me in the face.

"Hey, fucker! Watch it." I lunged forward to rip it off.

Kellita tugged me back.

"Oh, sorry," Lucky replied, his eyes saying he was anything but.

"No, you're not," I snarled.

Kellita snickered at our exchange.

Lucky stepped closer to Reason, guiding her away with a, "This way, beautiful."

"Shit, I'll follow you anywhere, Irish angel," Reason's husky voice replied.

My wolf snarled and rattled his cage, displeased when they disappeared.

"Really?" I glared at Kellita. "When did you start hiring male angels?"

She shrugged. "I'm trying something new to attract more female patrons."

"Well, I don't like it," I groused.

"Him," she interjected. "You don't like *him*... Lucky. I mean, I can't blame you. We don't call him Lucky for nothing. The man makes cunts wet without even trying." She paused. "And it seems he has his sights set on your date."

I arched a brow. "If he knows what's good for him, he'll leave her alone, or you'll have a wingless angel," I replied frigidly. "You know what? I'm done talking to you."

I started to walk away, but she tugged me back once more.

"I'm not done with you, Jackal. I have something serious to chat about." Her eyes narrowed as she bristled with anger.

Immediately, I focused on Kellita. I knew her personality well from years of being friends. This was Worried Kellita.

"What's going on?" I pulled her over into a secluded corner.

"I'm being stalked," she blurted out.

"You think—"

"Don't even mention his name," she finished with a shiver and a haunted look in her eyes. "I came to New York for a fresh start and thought, for once in my life, I could be happy and safe. But I feel it in my bones. Someone or something is watching me."

"Why didn't you tell me sooner?"

Kellita was the closest thing I had to a little sister, and I would give my life to protect her.

She shrugged. "Because I know you already have a lot on your plate with finding Light. I didn't want to distract you with my sordid skeletons."

"Don't worry about it. I'll contact my sources and see what I can find out. Okay?"

She nodded. "Thank you." Her lips curled up into a smile. "So what's the deal with you and..."

"Reason," I informed. "She's Oskar Orlov's daughter."

She arched a well-groomed brow. "Vampire?"

"Hybrid."

"Well, I like her." She touched my arm. "Does she know she's your mate?"

I was done with denying the truth, but I had no intention of claiming Reason. "No. And I'm not about to tell her or claim her." *Or risk losing her.* I'd been down that mate road before, and I wasn't about to do it again.

Her head cocked to the side. "Uh-huh." Her eyes narrowed, and she got a vertical wrinkle between her eyebrows. "That's your loss, Jackal." Her lips pursed slightly.

I glared at her.

She defensively held up her hands. "I'm not about to try and convince you that you're making a big mistake by not claiming her. That's your fucking cross to bear. Now, if I were you, I'd hustle my ass over to your table before Lucky sinks his claws into your mate." She winked and then walked away.

Just thinking about that idiot putting the moves on Reason had me storming into the open space with couches and tables on both sides leading up to a bar along the wall. My eyes panned across the area, stopping on the large, plush U-shaped communal couch anchoring the space. She wasn't there.

What the hell?

Then I spotted Lucky and Reason sitting side by side in a booth tucked into a secluded and cozy corner. My fists clenched when I saw one of his gigantic wings curled around her body way too intimately while his other hand pointed out items on the menu in her hand.

Oh, fuck no. I'm going to tear his damn wings off and make them a trophy for my living room wall.

Gritting my teeth, I nearly knocked over some patrons in my haste to get over to Reason. Finally reaching them, I snapped, "Get up," looking pointedly at Lucky.

Lucky slid out right away, making his wings disappear. "Sorry, man. I was just seeing what our pretty vampire desired"—his eyes challenged me—"from the menu."

Wait, when did she become our *pretty vampire?*

I nudged him aside and slid into the booth, taking the exact spot he'd just vacated. "I'll have a Jack on the rocks."

"I'll have a Grey Goose and tonic," Reason added while moving to the opposite end of the booth, as if she couldn't wait to get away from me.

What the hell is this about?

"And you'll consider what we talked about?" Lucky prodded her.

She smiled wryly and spoke softly, unruffled, and clearly, "Maybe." She winked at him.

I frowned at her.

"So what would you like to eat?" Lucky asked, eyes focused on Reason.

"Hmm... everything looks so delicious," she replied. The restaurant was loud, but her voice hung in the air.

"It sure does," Lucky commented, practically undressing her with his eyes.

"Lucky, you're this close"—I put my index and forefinger together—"to getting torn apart."

She rolled her eyes. "I'll have the lobster with crushed pota-toes," she ordered. "Oh, what the hell? I'm starving. Also, bring me the dry-rubbed scallops with polenta."

"Excellent choice," Lucky replied with a wink. Then he inspected me with cold eyes. "And you want the grass-fed New York strip steak with potatoes."

Reason laughed before saying, "How did you know that? Are you a telepathic angel?"

"Nope. He's a regular. The girls talk about him all the time. I guess because they know exactly what he likes," Lucky said snidely before striding away.

Fucking snitch. Yes, I'm going to come back here after I drop Reason home and rip his fucking wings off.

She eyed me with amusement. "So you're a regular here." It was a statement, not a question. Her eyes trailed over a scantily clad waitress who finger-waved at me before heading over to the bar with an exaggerated bump and grind of her hips. "Well, now I know what type of women you're into." She picked up her glass filled with water and sipped while looking around.

"I doubt it," I muttered, taking a moment to drink her in.

Her hair was pulled back into a casual ponytail, and if she was wearing makeup, I couldn't see it. She was all smooth skin and long eyelashes. In her left ear, she had a diamond stud in the lobe and two small gold rings around the helix. And she had two tattoos I could see—an *I Love New York* on her inner left arm and a vividly inked bumblebee tattoo on her right wrist.

"What's the significance of the bumblebee tattoo?" I asked.

Her eyes snapped over to stare into mine. "It reminds me to slow down and to enjoy life because it's precious and sweet."

Damn.

With every word she uttered, I was slowly sinking into the abyss of her uncomplicated aura. Continuing my survey, the clichés piled up like a traffic accident. Her voice was smoky and distinctive. Lips plump—bitable—and nose characterful and assertive. Her wide-spaced hazel eyes were intelligent and a little enigmatic.

"So what were you and Lucky talking about?" I asked, infusing a fake air of nonchalance.

She took a long sip of water, peering at me over the rim of her glass. "He asked me out to dinner." Her voice was a raspy frequency in the air.

"And you're actually considering it?" I barked.

"I like him." Her lips pursed.

My body tensed, and my inner wolf snarled.

"But I'm not romantically interested in Lucky. My days of sexual hook-ups are over," she finished.

My muscles relaxed but tensed up again when my inner beast yelled, *Claim her now!*

"I'm done with men who are only interested in my body. It's the reason I've been celibate."

I snorted. "No sex? How's that been going for you?"

She held her hands out, palms up, and smiled with a what-do-you-think shrug. "I get horny. I'm human and a woman. I want to have sex. But I won't settle. I will wait indefinitely if I have to. I've been screwed over enough times to know that waiting for Mr. Forever is fucking better than settling for Mr. Right Now."

And then, for some insane reason, I was about to grab her hands and tell her what I wanted. Making it a demand, an assertion, rather than a request. *Reason, my soul and wolf yearn to be your Mr. Forever. You're the one woman who could very well be my salvation.*

But I was scared as fuck to take the leap and claim her as mine. So instead of giving in to my emotions and inner beast, I latched onto the one truth in my clusterfuck of a world—Reason was safer without me in her life.

"The one thing we," Reason uttered, "Others have in our favor is the whole true-mate thing. We recognize our soul mates immediately. There's no indecisiveness, like humans. No games. The process is pretty cut and dry. The person is either your mate or just another fuck buddy available to bide the time with until —or *if*—you ever find your other half."

"True mates..." I couldn't help the snort that escaped. "The ultimate double-edged sword. A curse and a blessing." I took a quick sip of water to relieve my suddenly dry throat. The topic of true mates always seemed to do that to me.

Reason arched a brow. "A curse?" Her voice, as always, was a little sandy, as if she'd been singing all day.

I rattled off the list of things from my perspective that made having a true mate a pain in the ass. "Ryker hasn't had a good night's sleep or a decent meal since Light got kidnapped by the Shadows. He's been snapping at everyone. Shit, he's a fucking mess without her. She's his other half, and his disposition will only get worse if she dies during this whole fucking mess." I shook my head in disgust. "And don't let me even start on the depression that will last forever and the bitterness that will linger."

"What do you mean by *bitterness*?" she asked, putting a finger to her chin.

"Resentment because the universe brought him his true match, only to cruelly snatch her away."

"You sound like you're speaking from experience."

I could practically see her wheels turning with unasked questions. I'd noticed one of her tells was she would bite the inside of her cheek when she was becoming nervous.

Shit, I said too much.

"Well? Are you going to elaborate?" she inquired.

"Here are your drinks."

So engrossed in our conversation, we were both startled by the presence of the server with our drinks on a silver tray. Swiftly, he placed them in front of us before scurrying away.

Reason took a sip of her drink before asking, "Well? How do you know about the mating thing?"

Why can't she let this shit go?

"That's personal," I said aloofly.

"So I'm not allowed to ask you personal questions?"

I sighed heavily. "How would you like it if I started prying into your personal life?"

She shrugged. "I don't have anything to hide. Ask away."

My eyes narrowed. "What's the deal with you and your father's enforcer Stefan?" My stomach twisted at the thought of her and that fucker being romantically linked. I'd heard a lot of shit about Stefan's exploits through intel from Others, and nothing about him seemed good.

She pursed her lips before saying, "He's the consort my father has chosen for me to marry."

"You're getting married?" I sputtered.

"Yes, to Stefan." Her face was not quite like thunder, but certainly held an overcast expression—unsmiling, eyes blank.

My heart raced. My inner wolf growled with displeasure while rattling the cage I'd contained him in. "He doesn't seem like your type."

Shit, please don't let him be your type.

We're her type. Tell her. Now, my wolf snapped.

She placed her fingers on the table. "And what the hell do you know about my type, Jackal?"

"Darling, I know Stefan isn't it." I refused to back down. My alpha dominance urged me to push her into admitting what we both already knew—she was mine, regardless if I claimed her or not.

She blew out a calming breath. "I'm not going to bullshit you. He's not, but according to my dad and coven, he's a more than suitable match. So... in essence, he's my Mr. Right Now."

"Sounds... cold and calculating."

"Well, isn't that what shifters believe vampires are? Cold and calculating? That we know nothing about love? That we marry for power and prestige? And we fuck around like rabbits to kill the boredom?"

She lifted an eyebrow. It was her trademark I-dare-you-to-say-something-to-the-contrary glare. But I couldn't.

"Reason, you and I know there are way too many stereotypes and prejudices on both sides—shifter and vampire. And that shit will never change, no matter how much we wish it would. But right now, all I really care about is what *you* want."

Her eyes darted away and then back. "Jackal, I'm Princess Orlov. My duty is to my father and the coven."

"A fucking bullshit title? You don't need it. You're beautiful and smart. You can turn your back on the coven and make a life anywhere."

"Jackal, I'm a hybrid. I have one foot in the human world and one in the vampire world, and neither will accept me."

"That doesn't mean you have to accept that archaic vampire shit."

"That's so easy for you to say." She leaned forward with challenge in her eyes. "Tell me, shifter, what happens to wolf-shifters without a pack?"

"They eventually go feral," I replied simply.

"Well, hybrid vampires get killed by their own kind. You see, I'm considered to be a blight by most and prey by all. Frankly, the only person keeping me alive is my father, but he won't live forever. And then what?" With some lip pursing and a calculated shrug, she muttered, "Now it's your turn to lay yourself bare. Who's Josie?"

I stiffened. "Where did you hear that name?"

"I'm psychic," she replied bluntly.

I arched a brow. "Hardly."

"From you, while you were in my bed." She took a sip of her drink, giving me the evil eye.

"Shit, that's fucked up."

"Very."

I gulped my drink, hoping to ignore her question about Josie, but the lawyer in her would not let it go unanswered.

"So?" she snapped.

"I don't want to fucking talk about it."

She drummed her fingernails against the table. "Unfortunately for you, I do."

"What's with you, woman? You push—"

"And you run." She leaned forward. "You know me by now. I'm not the type to stew silently or go sulk in some damn corner. Or worse, not ask the hard questions. I keep it real. And I want to know; who's Josie? And why does the mere mention of her name have you so fucking shaken up?"

Anger raced through my veins. "Reason, you think I know you, but I don't."

"Jackal, my life is an open book. And my past is behind me, like a ponytail. So ask away."

"Dredging up the past is not a good thing for me. It's like ripping open stitches of a barely healed wound. It's painful, bloody, and not something I like to do."

My inner wolf growled impatiently, *Just tell her.*

Reason's face transformed into a neutral mask. She was shutting down, and something about her closing up emotionally bothered the fuck out of me. So I conceded to my wolf.

"Josie was my mate." I swallowed over the lump of emotions in my throat. "And she was killed by vampires."

Her mouth opened and shut. "I'm so sorry." She quickly shifted along the seat to move closer to me, her leg now pressed against mine.

"Losing my mate and"—my voice cracked, and I quickly cleared it—"unborn child cut deep. One minute, I had everything, and the next, I lost it all in the blink of an eye."

She pressed a soft hand on top of mine.

"She was slaughtered to get back at me." The truth sliced like a knife. "I worked Special Forces for years. Doing things I can't even fucking talk about. Let's just say, I was given orders to complete missions that made me a lot of fucking enemies. But instead of them coming after me to seek their revenge, they wanted to send a deadly message to me and the military agency I worked for. So they killed Josie. And I spent years hunting them down and killing most of them."

She threaded her fingers through mine and squeezed. "Damn, I'm so sorry."

Lucky and another server approached the table with a tray laden with food.

"Lobster with crushed potatoes and dry-rubbed scallops with polenta," Lucky announced as the server grandly set the plates down before Reason. "And a grass-fed New York strip steak with potatoes." He set the one plate in front of me. "Enjoy." He finished with a bow of his head.

Lucky beamed at Reason, totally ignoring me. "Would you like another drink?"

"No. Too much alcohol causes me to make bad decisions," she answered with a wink.

He eyed me.

"Nothing for me," I snapped before he and the server roamed away.

Reason dug into her polenta, sticking a forkful into her mouth. Her pink tongue flicked out to lick at the droplet of sauce on her bottom lip. My eyes followed the movement, and my cock pulsated with the thought of how her plump lips would feel wrapped around my girth while I fucked her mouth.

"Stop that," Reason whispered.

"Stop what?" I cut into my steak before shoving it into my mouth.

"Looking at me like you want to spread me across this table and fuck me like a recently released prisoner." She exhaled loudly. "You don't find me attractive, shifter. You despise the vampire blood running through my veins because of what happened to your mate and unborn child. I get it."

"Quite the opposite, Reason." I swallowed hard. "I find everything about you to be sheer perfection."

"Except for the fact that I'm a vampire."

My heart thudded at the sultry smokiness of her voice.

"It's complicated."

She scowled. "Then explain it to me like I'm a fucking two-year-old."

I growled impatiently. *How can I verbalize my greatest fear? That I spent years avoiding relationships and any romantic attachments because I was terrified of loving so deeply again? That I couldn't take another mate because those vampire fuckers who murdered Josie and my child were waiting and watching for the opportune time to climb out of the darkness and snatch my happiness and mate away from me... again? That I spent so many years crawling in and out of bed with one woman after another with not a care in the world because I knew there was no chance of ever finding another possible mate?*

Until I'd met her.

The infuriating vampire was the only woman who made my wolf sit up and take notice. She was the only woman my beast wanted—no, needed. But I'd be damned if I watched her die. It would fucking tear me apart... and this time, there would be no coming back from the edge of insanity.

"Here's what I can't figure out. Why are you still single?" I asked. "You're ravishing, radiant, sublime, and good enough to eat."

"Men need attention and nourishment," she explained. "That little stroke of the ego that gets them by every now and then. I give it to my father and friends. I give it to my work, but I won't give it to a man right now."

"Why not?"

"All my life, I've had to be so conscious about people. What they say and why they want to be with me. Why they want to sleep with me. It makes me very guarded and protective. Over the years, I've learned the hard way that most people don't give a shit about me. They just want to use me to get close to the meanest and most powerful vampire in the Northeast. My father." She paused. "So as you can imagine, I have mixed feelings about men and love. Love is nothing but a whim. An emotion that can be manipulated."

My chest tightened. "That's a bleak way to think about it."

"How else can it be defined?"

"It's a longing. A need to be with that person for the rest of your life. The recognition that there is no one like her, and when you are around her... or not"—I grabbed her hand, pressing it against my lips—"you think about her constantly. Even though, deep down, you know"—I gently laid her hand on the table —"she deserves better. More than you can ever give because you're broken. That you lost a piece of yourself so long ago that it can't be found again."

"And that's where I beg to disagree. A heart can be mended— if you're brave enough to take a leap and allow a person in." She expectantly stared at me.

I remained silent, undecided on how to proceed.

Reason looked slightly disappointed but moved on. "The funny thing is, even with the hard and painful lessons I've learned from my uncanny ability to fall for men who don't want me, deep inside, I hope for the best. I always look for that little bit of good and that potential." She studied me. "Waiting for it to blossom into something that is true and beautiful. And when that happens... maybe I'll be brave enough to leap. Opening my heart to a man who loves me just as hard as I love him."

And for the first time in my life, I felt like a coward for my inability to leap, claiming her as mine. I just wasn't willing to throw caution to the wind, risking my heart again.

No, the man Reason wanted and needed would never be me.

And that brutal truth hurt like a motherfucker.

❦ 9 ❦

REASON

MY BETRAYING lady bits quivered deliciously from the annoying presence of Jackal's large hand pressed against my lower back while guiding me through the alleyway maze, away from Angels.

My cunt's mutiny was just another reminder that my unofficial first date with him hadn't exactly gone according to my plan. Frankly, I was emotionally torn and fucking angered by Jackal's coolness toward me now. It seemed as if our candid discussion during dinner about our pasts and perspectives about love, life, and relationships had only driven a deeper wedge between us instead of bringing us closer.

Normally, I wasn't a quitter when it came to going after what I wanted, which was Jackal. But the signs were obvious. It was time to wave the white flag on the whole Jackal predicament and move on to greener pastures.

Finally reaching the wider section of the alleyway that opened to the street, I skidded to a stop. Whirling around to face him, I pasted on a smile. "Look, Jackal, dinner was nice, but you and I know that's all it was."

I patted him on the shoulder. His eyes flicked down to my hand and then back to my face.

"So let's just say good night right here, and I'll catch a cab."

Simultaneously lugging my leather handbag over my head, letting it slide across my shoulder like a messenger bag, I finished with, "See you around."

When I turned on my heel, my body stiffened as two men appeared, blocking the only path out of the alleyway. "What the fuck is this?"

Jackal growled low and deep before tugging me behind his massive back. "Reason, don't move. I got this."

"Jesus, are they trying to rob us?" I croaked.

It was well after midnight, and nothing good ever happened this late at night, despite the fact that we were in the nice part of Manhattan.

"Back the fuck up and walk away, or shit's going to get real bloody... for you." Jackal's dark tone rang with deadly promise.

"I don't think so, shifter. We've got you outnumbered," a man's voice answered, followed by a chorus of men's laughter.

Anchoring my hands on each side of Jackal's narrow waist, I peeked around his body.

Oh shit. This is not good.

Three more men had joined the initial two. Now there was a wall, five men deep, effectively trapping us in the alleyway. My hand slipped into my bag, fingers wrapping around my Taser. Not that I didn't trust that Jackal could handle the situation. The man was built like an MMA fighter and was mean like a rattlesnake. But I just wasn't the wait-around-for-a-man-on-a-white-horse-to-save-the-day kind of chick. I was a fighter.

As one, the men moved toward us.

The one with a mop of dirty-blond hair said, "We were sent to take care of you, shifter. And we're not leaving until the job is done." He sneered with fangs peeking from his top lip.

I gasped. *What are rogue vampires doing in Dad's territory?*

The New York vampire community was so small that everyone knew each other, and these men were outsiders.

Now I was pissed. These vampires were blatantly thumbing their noses at Dad's authority. All vampires, regardless of what territory they resided in, knew the most important vampire covenant rule—thou shall not come into a vampire king's or queen's territory without damn permission.

I stepped out from behind Jackal to stand by his side. "Do you fuckers have a death wish?"

"Jesus, woman," Jackal snapped. "Why can't you follow simple instructions?" His eyes flashed angrily before he gave me a light push, motioning for me to move behind him, but I refused to budge.

"Shifter," I hissed, "will you just let me help defuse this situation?"

Ignoring me, he took a step forward. "Give her safe passage out of here, and then we can handle this shit like men."

Heaven, preserve me. Men and their macho, testosterone-infused bullshit.

"I'll gladly let the lady go," the leader said serenely with a mock bow. "Her father paid us to kill your whole pack. Starting with you. She has nothing to do with our assignment."

My body froze. "That's impossible," I croaked. *Why would Dad do something so crazy?*

"Then come and get me," Jackal retorted easily.

"Kill him," their leader ordered.

One man surged forward, knocking me out of the way. My body slammed against the brick wall before sliding down onto my ass with a hard thump. I struggled to get to my feet, watching Jackal pick the man up, effortlessly pressing him over his head and tossing him feet away like a bag of garbage. The sound of the man's body slamming against the ground with bones crunching pierced the air.

Utter chaos broke out when all four men swooped down on Jackal with a flurry of kicks and punches. Jackal shook them off, grabbing one man and twisting his arm in an unnatural angle before a howling scream filled the air. Grunts and shrieks followed as Jackal commenced putting the beatdown on their asses with a precision that was terrifying, vicious, and bloody.

The man is a fucking killing machine.

My heart pounded when I saw one of them pull out a knife, aiming for his back. My mind kicked into gear. Digging into my designer handbag, I pulled out my Taser before zapping the man. He yelped before dropping to the ground, convulsing like a fish out of water.

"Reason, run," Jackal grunted while choking one of the men.

"I'm helping here," I grumbled.

"You little..." one of the men snarled before shoving me headfirst into the wall.

The Taser dropped and skittered across the ground. The skin on my forehead stung from the bang against the bricks. Now I was pissed.

Spinning around to face him, I screamed, "You asshole!" before kneeing him in the groin so hard he squealed like a pig, doubling over. Taking the opening, I hauled back and punched him in the face. "Ouch!" I cried from the impact as the pain raced up my hand.

Glancing around, I assessed the damage from Jackal's commando-gone-crazy rampage. All the men were either unconscious or rolling around on the ground, groaning in pain.

Jackal was glaring at me like he wanted to strangle me to death. I rolled my eyes. The bastard didn't have a scratch on him, nor did he look like he'd even broken a sweat.

Meanwhile, I felt like I had just been in a cage fight and lost. Blood dripped down my forehead. My knee was sore. My knuckles were bruised. And, goddammit, one of my favorite red-bottom shoes was missing a heel.

"Great, Jackal. Just fucking great," I snapped. "These shoes cost a damn fortune." I whipped them off, stuffing them into my handbag. "You, Jack Alagona, are a menace to society and a fucking bad luck charm."

"How the hell is this my fault?"

"It just is. Everywhere you go, someone wants to kick your ass or kill you."

Spotting my Taser on the ground, I snatched it up and was about to shove it into my handbag when one of the men rolling around in agony yelled in my direction, "You traitorous vampire bitch!"

"Didn't your mother ever teach you damn manners?" I hissed, marching over to him.

"Fuck you," he spit.

Digging out my extra cartridge, I loaded it into the Taser and aimed it at his chest. "I live for the simple things... like how much this shit is going to hurt you." I shot quickly and precisely, watching with glee as his body convulsed with involuntary muscle spasms. "Yes, asshole, writhe."

"Darling, I'm glad I'm on your side," Jackal mumbled.

"You"—I pointed a finger at him—"not another word, or I'll load up my Taser again and aim for your cock."

"Now why would you want to do some crazy shit like that?" he snapped.

"I warned you." I started searching in my bag for another cartridge.

"Come on, woman." He snatched my hand, dragging me out of the alleyway.

We didn't speak a word until we reached his parked car.

Pushing me against his vehicle, he grabbed my face, inspecting my forehead. "Reason, when I say get the fuck out of here, I mean it. What the hell is wrong with you?"

I raised my chin in a gesture of defiance and met his gaze. "Is that a thank you? Because it sounds like you're being an ungrateful bastard."

"I just can't stand seeing you get hurt." He closely watched me, the expression in his eyes making me feel precious and beautiful.

My heart thumped hard in my chest. *Damn, he cares about me.*

He reached out and grazed my face with the back of his hand. "You have a cut on your forehead." He slightly stepped back, inspecting the rest of me. "Look at your hand. It looks like you were bare-knuckle fighting. Shit, woman. You're a damn mess."

"Thank you for the compliment. Now, if you'll excuse me, I need to go home to take a long, hot bath and a couple aspirins." I skirted past him, heading to the passenger side.

He snatched me from behind, pressing my back against his chest. "Let me take care of you." His voice was a velvet whisper against my ear.

A shiver ran down my spine. No matter how hard I tried to stay mad at him, I just couldn't. He made my insides feel like jelly.

"I can take care of myself, Jackal." Instead of pulling away, my traitorous body relaxed into him. "Now let go."

"Only if you let me take care of your wounds, and then I'll go away."

With an aggrieved sigh, I said, "Jesus, you're such a pain in the ass. Okay, but don't expect me to be good company. I'm feeling grumpy and a tad bit emotionally raw."

He opened the passenger door for me, and I slid in and sank against the cool leather seat, closing my eyelids. Then I remembered the most important tidbit from the alley attack. My eyes snapped open. I pulled out my cell and dialed Dad. It went straight to voice mail. Strange. It never did that.

I tapped out a text.

Call me now!

Jackal slid into the vehicle and pulled away.

"Explain," I commanded.

"Explain what?" he grumbled, racing through the streets.

"Why would my dad put a hit on your whole pack?"

"You might not want to admit it, but the man is certifiably insane. He's never cared for shifters or the permanent peace pact. Maybe he's just had enough of pretending like he actually gives a shit."

"No, that doesn't make sense. Yes, the animosity between the Orlov coven and shifters has been thinly veiled. But the temporary truce has been working for years. By sending those men to kill you, he's just openly declared war on shifters. My father is way more covert than that." I bit my bottom lip. This whole situation between the shifters and vampires was spiraling out of control. "Plus, he promised me he would help Ryker get Light back. He never breaks his promises."

"Bullshit! He breaks them all the time, Reason."

I shook my head. "Not to me, he doesn't."

Contrary to what Jackal thought, I wasn't naive about the kind of man my dad was. He was cruel, calculating, manipulative, and downright emotionless most of the time. But the one constant I could always count on when it came to our relationship was his promises to me. And his word was his bond.

I WAS STARTLED AWAKE BY THE WARMTH OF JACKAL'S HAND gripping my thigh, and I groaned. My thigh felt like it was on fire from back-to-back cardio boxing classes.

"Are you okay?" he asked.

"Okay as I can be." I rubbed my eyes, realizing we'd arrived at my townhouse. "Just a little bruised, but that will pass in a day or two."

"Don't vampires heal quickly?"

"I'm a hybrid. My healing process is slower, but it gets the job done." I started to unbuckle my seat belt.

"Let me do that." He hustled out of the car, coming around to my side. He opened the door and removed the belt.

I prepared to hop out but winced from the throbbing pain in my knee. He swooped down and picked me up as if I weighed nothing.

"Jackal! Put me the hell down. I'm not a baby."

"But you were banged around quite a bit." He slammed the door with one hand. "I'll feel better if I just carry you inside."

Digging into my handbag, I pulled out my keys, handing

them over. "If you insist." I tried not to dwell on it, but it wasn't a bad deal, being fussed over by him.

It didn't take Jackal long to leap up the stairs and open the door. Kicking it closed behind us, he locked it before striding across the floor. He placed me on top of the granite kitchen countertop before moving over to the sink. Turning on the water, he wet a towel before marching back over to me.

"Spread your legs," he demanded, low and rough. "I need to get in."

I parted them slightly.

"Wider. I'm a big man."

I stifled a giggle. Jesus, everything he uttered sounded like a sexual proposition.

"How big?" I couldn't resist asking.

A smile twitched across his lips. "How big do you want it, vampire?"

"God, we sound like a bad porno movie."

He grabbed my thighs, spreading them indecently wide before stepping in between them. My core twitched, and I knew his shifter nose could smell how aroused I was. But I wasn't the only one. I felt the hardness of his manhood pressing against the apex of my thighs.

"This might sting a little," Jackal growled before he began to clean my forehead with gentle motions.

"Ouch," I complained.

"Oh, suck it up, vampire." His eyes narrowed. "It's not as bad as I thought it was. It won't leave a scar. Just a little scratch. You'll live."

He leaned against me with way more closeness than needed, and I smelled the spiciness of his cologne. I felt the thumping of his heart, and it was racing a mile a minute... just like mine.

"Really? Already knew that."

"Your fighting skills are horrible," he rumbled. "If it wasn't for that Taser, your injuries would have been worse. Why don't you know how to fight?"

I grabbed the cloth from him. "I think I held my own, shifter."

"That's not good enough. When fighting Others, you have to be ready to kill or be killed."

"I know that, but I can't fight like that."

"Can't? Like you can't break a fucking nail?" He sounded so incredulous.

"Literally, I don't know shit about fighting Others," I said simply.

Looking mystified, he stared at me. "I don't get it."

"Vampire princesses don't fight. That's what the coven's enforcers are for. Female vampires are sheltered, coddled, and treated like porcelain dolls." I huffed out a breath, struggling with how much of my humiliating pretentious upbringing I should reveal. "Oh God, this is so embarrassing."

He grabbed my chin, rubbing a callused thumb over my bottom lip. "I'm listening," he said before his fingers fell away.

Without thinking, I blurted out, "Groomers."

"What?" He arched a brow.

Oh, fuck it. I was about to reveal a part of vampire culture that most people outside of covens knew nothing about.

"Groomers are experts in all aspects of keeping a female vampire happy. They're vampires assigned to a princess from the day she's born. I was taught about the hierarchy of each coven and vampire rules. The vampires' archaic language. How to eat with the right utensils. What to wear for each ceremony. How to pleasure my future consort."

"Pleasure your mate? Vampires finally got something right." He wiggled his brows.

"Do you want to hear this or not?" I shoved him, but it was like pushing against a brick wall.

"Darling, you had me at *pleasure*."

I rolled my eyes heavenward. "Anyway... all princesses are also assigned an enforcer detail, which they keep for their entire lives. I had one until I graduated from law school. I convinced my father I didn't need a detail, but of course, there was one caveat. I had to stay in New York City and work for him."

"Holy shit."

Tone just as flat as ever, I said, "Yeah, holy shit. And for years, I've begged my father to get one of his enforcers to train me in fighting Others."

"And?"

"He said no. So I've secretly been paying for self-defense classes. The instructor is human, so it's not the same as learning how to take down Others, but I make do." I bit my lower lip. "Hey, I have a great idea. Why don't you teach me some self-defense moves?"

Jackal snorted. "Way too much work. You're too prissy to get your hands dirty."

I jumped down. "Let's go."

He stiffened and his eyes narrowed. "And do what?"

"Fight."

"You're no match for me, Reason." He shrugged one shoulder.

I refused to let him intimidate me. With my chin tilted at a stubborn angle, I held my ground. "Try me, asshole."

A muscle twitched beneath Jackal's left eye. "And break the great Oskar Orlov's daughter? Nope. I don't need all that noise when he finds out."

"I want to learn. Look, it'll be between us."

"Nope." He started walking toward my refrigerator. "What do you want to drink?"

"Okay, how about this? If I get you on the floor, then you have to promise to train me. If not, no hard feelings, and I'll let this whole topic drop."

Jackal turned around and stared at me. "You're so fucking stubborn."

"That's what I've been told."

He walked past me, stopping in the middle of the living room. "Bring it, vampire." He wiggled his fingers.

Instead of charging forward, like he expected, I swayed toward him. He smiled smugly. Standing before him, I kneed him hard in the groin. He fell forward in pain. I shoved his head back, causing his massive body to teeter backward. Riding the momentum, I leaped onto him, and he fell onto his back with a thud.

Straddling his waist, I grinned down at him. "So what time do we train tomorrow?"

He growled, rolling over and pinning me under his body. "That was real dirty, vampire. I like it."

My breath stopped at the intense hunger in his eyes as he stroked a finger down my cheek, trailing to my bottom lip. I jerked at the contact.

"Don't move," he ordered.

His hand slid to my jaw, and his head tilted before his lips settled across my mouth. My breath caught. His grip on my jaw contracted. His tongue slid between my teeth. The kiss was long and deep—the stamp of his possession. No one had ever kissed me like this.

Jesus, I'm so fucked.

He sucked my tongue into his mouth. My stomach contracted as a rush of heat flooded my entire body. My hands wrapped tightly around his lean waist, and lust curled deep in my needy place. Jackal was slowly crumbling my resolve to remain emotionally detached. He pulled his lips away from mine but kept his hand firmly controlling my face. He smiled like the devil reincarnated.

I arched up, my teeth grazing his throat, before I inched back ever so slightly, stroking his face with the backs of my fingers, going from his cheek to his full lips. As my fingers caressed his mouth, he opened his lips and licked my knuckles with just a quick flick of his warm tongue. A feeling of excitement fluttered like butterflies in the pit of my stomach. The sensation ratcheted my emotions like a kid on a roller coaster.

He fastened his mouth on mine, and my clit thumped against

my panties with everything inside me shattering from his kiss. My hands desperately clutched his shoulders to anchor myself. My soft lips were on his hard ones. A stinging nip of his teeth made me open my mouth, and he plunged in, his tongue stroking mine. My nails dug into his muscular shoulders as searing need burned between my legs.

Nudging my legs farther apart, I rubbed my sex across the bulge in his pants. Our kiss became deeper. I brushed against his hard-on with a slow and steady motion. In one sinuous movement, he released me and inched his way down my body. In the blink of an eye, my legs were hooked over his shoulders. He settled his face in the V of my thighs, pushing my panties aside before voraciously going after the damp petals of my center.

His tongue lapped me from my clit to the end of my cleft. He swirled his tongue around my clit, repeatedly flicking it, and then sank it inside me. I panted, my hips arching. Jackal growled a long, low snarl, a sound that turned me on, making me insane. Holding me still, he unrelentingly fucked me with his wicked tongue. I hissed as he worked me into a frenzy, using sensual licks. His mouth constantly teased my opening.

Showing me no damn mercy, he flicked my swollen nub until I screamed, "Oh my fucking God!" I bucked as he continued to bathe me with his mouth.

He thrust two fingers into my trembling channel, curving them inside me, while pressing his thumb on my clit so his hand was clamped around me. I moaned as I clenched those fingers tight. He growled again.

My body stilled, allowing my mind to catch up with my emotions. I couldn't do this. I refused to go back down that one-night-stand road.

I want better. No, I deserve better.

My hands eased down to his head, stilling him. "Jackal," I whispered.

He raised his head, peering at me with sharp eyes. My juices glistened on his lips like liquor, filling me with perverse satisfaction and possessiveness.

"We can't do this," I finished.

Pressing his forehead against my thigh, he mumbled something I couldn't comprehend before quickly rolling off me onto his back. His breath was rapid, as if he were trying to get himself under control, and he threw his forearms across his face.

I needed to move. Watching him would only prolong the torture of wanting something *more* with Jackal. Rolling onto my knees, I wobbled to my feet.

"I'm going to take a shower." I bit my bottom lip, staring at his prone body. "Please don't make this any harder on me, Jackal. Just be gone when I come out." Turning on my heel, I stormed into my bedroom.

Peeling off my clothes, I stepped into the master bathroom. Turning on my steam shower, I jumped in, quickly washing my hair and body. Stepping out, I grabbed a fluffy white towel and was drying off when the bathroom door burst open. And Jackal was standing at the threshold, gawking at my dripping wet body.

I wrapped the towel around myself. "Ever heard of knocking?"

"Sorry, but I'm not leaving until I do what I came here for." He shook the bottle of hydrogen peroxide.

I took a long, deep audible breath. "Do it and then leave."

He nodded with his lips pressed together. Marching forward, he picked me up, plopping me onto the granite countertop. He dabbed a cotton swab against my knee while I stiffly sat there.

"Reason... I want you more than my next breath, but I can't give you what you really need."

"And that is?" My heart raced.

"A man who can give you forever." His eyes locked with mine. "And that man isn't me." He swallowed. "With Josie, I loved and lost. Frankly, I'm not strong enough to go through that shit again. But that doesn't have to stop you and me from enjoying the here and now. Just with no commitment or obligation."

No commitment or obligation? With those four words, he simultaneously broke and steeled my heart.

"It's okay. I understand," I said simply. "But I'm not settling for less than all of you. Now get the fuck out. And don't come back to me until you're ready to give me forever."

He stared at me, stunned. Then his jaw tightened before he placed the bottle of peroxide on the counter and stormed out of the bathroom.

I couldn't move. Every fiber of my body was numb.

I felt defeated. Worthless.

I wanted to run after him. To yell and scream at him for denying our connection. For him forcing me to feel like shit. For the fact that he didn't even feel I was worth pushing past the fear caused by his past loss.

And for the first time in years, I pulled back the mask of neutrality, allowing tears of despair to fall down my cheeks. Mourning the loss of him and me.

❦ 10 ❦

REASON

JOGGING up the stairs of the train station, I landed in the middle of the crowded Manhattan sidewalk.

Damn, I'm late.

Not that I was particularly thrilled when Jackal had texted me early this morning about meeting up today for our first How to Survive & Win an Others Apocalypse Defensive Training Session. But I refused to let Jackal think I was afraid to meet him after last night.

Orienting myself to my surroundings, I weaved in and out of the heavy throng of New York pedestrians. Every so often, I would catch myself glancing over my shoulder, searching for the protection detail I'd ditched an hour ago.

My mouth tightened with irritation. I would have arrived sooner if it hadn't been for the time wasted shaking Dad's enforcers. As usual, he hadn't given a shit about my opinion and had assigned me a protection detail that trailed me after I left my place a couple hours ago. The crafty enforcers had forced me to ditch my SUV at a parking garage, and I'd had to hop a train just to get here.

Damn my life as a runaway princess.

I knew Dad was going to be pissed at me for eluding his

security. But as far as I was concerned, he was already livid with me for interfering with his planned assassination of Jackal last night.

What was one more item added to his Ax to Grind with Reason list?

Finally reaching the front of Ryker's headquarters, I marched across the marble floor, heading for the security desk.

"Can I help you?" the guard asked.

"Reason Orlov." I handed over my ID. "I'm here to see Jack Alagona."

He gave my ID a quick glance before handing it back. "Take the elevator. Fifth floor." He nodded to the left.

Walking toward the waiting elevator, I started formulating a strategy to make my encounter with Jackal as neutral as possible.

Stepping inside, I mumbled aloud, "This isn't rocket science. Jackal trains me. I walk away. We rinse and repeat until I'm done learning all I need from him, and then I kick his ass to the curb. End of story."

I wasn't too perfect to admit his rebuff had put a chink in my confidence.

Why am I even doing this after the shit that went down between us last night?

I sighed heavily. *Because I'm a glutton for punishment.*

I wanted Jackal desperately. But I couldn't go back to a life of crawling into bed to satisfy my body's sexual cravings. I needed a man to quench my spirit, mind, and body. And every cell in my body told me Jackal was the one. It just hurt like hell that he obviously didn't feel the same way about me.

My chest thudded from just remembering the ache in my heart after he'd left. Numbly, I'd went to bed, still tasting him on my lips and wanting his hot, hard shaft between my legs.

I snapped back to the present, my fists clenched at my sides. And me seeing Jackal so soon after our encounter would be self-inflicted emotional torture.

The elevator stopped, and the door opened to reveal a large

space. Jackal and Rip were sparring in the middle of the cushioned floor. I stepped out, observing the fighting action between the two. It was like watching a deadly ballet, the way their well-toned, muscled bodies twisted, dodged, kicked, and wrestled.

Jackal and Rip beat the ever-loving pulp out of each other for the duration of their fight. Jackal got rocked by a right hand from Rip but managed to regain his composure before peppering Rip with boxing combinations that rattled him. The fight had more twists than any other fight I could think of, with both men seemingly milliseconds away from victory multiple times.

I looked on like a deer caught in headlights. "Are they serious? They're fighting like they want to kill each other. Damn cocky wolf-shifters."

Rip swiftly flipped midair, avoiding Jackal's reach before landing on his feet. Then he proceeded to throw a series of punches. Rip kicked his leg out, extending from the hip, pausing with his leg suspended effortlessly midair, mere inches from Jackal's face. Jackal swiftly swung his treelike muscled arm, swatting his leg away with a vicious move.

Damn, I was completely turned on by a hot, sweaty, virile-looking Jackal.

Rip ran toward him, and Jackal sidestepped, landing a flying kick right into Rip's face that sent him tumbling to the ground. Then Jackal was on top of him, throwing hammer fists.

"I hope he's not planning on doing that to me," I mumbled under my breath.

In the middle of the fight, almost out of nowhere, Jackal forever solidified his badass credentials by making Rip submit with a choke hold made for high-level MMA.

"Give up?" Jackal barked.

Rip nodded and rolled away on the floor, flopping onto his back and breathing hard. "Asshole," he hissed.

"The biggest," Jackal replied before deftly standing.

Rip got to his feet and groaned. "I don't remember you being this fast or strong. Are you taking performance enhancers?"

Jackal snorted. "Never. It's all in the genes, dude."

Rip's eyes narrowed. "You mean it's all in the vampire blood."

Jackal watched me with impatience written all over his face. Today, he was wearing all black—loose black track pants, fitted black T-shirt, and black sneakers.

He examined me like I was a specimen under a microscope. I was happy I'd spared the time to put on tight yoga pants and a T-shirt with black steel-tipped boots.

Muscular forearms crossed in front of him while he stared pointedly at me. "Next session, get here on time. I don't like waiting around, Reason."

"Hello to you, too," I snapped. "How long is this session going to be? I have plans today," I spoke nonchalantly.

"With whom?" He rolled his shoulders.

"None of your business."

"It'd better not be Stefan." His eyes flashed a feral warning.

"And if it is?" I plodded forward, staring him up and down. I would be damned if I told him my plans involved getting home in time to primp for Dad's vampire gala that I was expected to attend tonight.

"I'll hunt him down and break his neck." His nostrils flared. A low rumbling started.

I rolled my eyes. "Calm down, caveman. You're worse than my father."

He scoffed. "Doubt it. Your father tried to kill me."

I playfully fluttered my eyelashes. "Oh, that."

"Kind of hard to forgive, don't you think?" He paused. "So did he tell you why he'd sent assassins to kill me?"

"I haven't talked to him yet."

Oddly, Dad had not returned any of my voice messages. Knowing him, he was probably sulking about me ruining his plan to kill Jackal.

"But I'll find out why."

"Strategy," he replied simply. "He'll pick off all the strongest packs, prides, and clans, and then he can retain and control this region without competition."

Stretching my arms behind my back to work out the kinks, I mulled over what he'd just said and then rejected it. "No, that's bullshit."

"No, vampire, that's a power move."

"Jackal, I know my dad. He's got plenty of power without chancing an all-out war. No, something else is going on. Shit within the coven is precarious, but no one is stupid enough to challenge him for power. And my dad's doing everything to keep the coven together, even if the Shadows are successfully waging a divide-and-conquer campaign. But I don't know... He's seemed abnormally distracted lately."

"If you ask me, your father is batshit crazy."

"Hey, he's just eccentric and stubborn." I scowled.

Jackal stared at me like I'd lost my mind. "You're delusional."

"Call it what you want. Now let's get going. I've got things to do." I arched a brow.

He glanced at the staff at his feet. "This is for you."

I walked up to him and picked it up. "Okay, what am I supposed to do with this?"

"It's a practice staff," he snapped.

I blinked in confusion. "And that means what?" I sounded frustrated, even to my own ears.

"It's exactly what the name implies. We practice with it."

I stared at him. "If you continue to act like a grade-A asshat, I'm going to punch you in the damn throat."

"Jesus, woman." He grabbed the staff out of my hand. "Stand back and watch." He thrust the staff forward and then swung it above his head, effortlessly spinning it around. The air menacingly whooshed around him.

Jamming my hands on my hips, I watched incredulously until he stopped moving. "You really expect me to do that?"

"Yes." He pushed the staff into my hand. "Today, I want you to practice using your senses when fighting. None of the bullshit you did last night. Not once did you know where the attackers were before they were all over you. You have to be aware of your opponent's location at all times. If you practice long enough, eventually, you will be able to anticipate their next move before they actually do it."

"If you say so."

"Okay, let's go," he snarled, picking up another staff and demonstrating the motions. "So it's left, right, left, and kick."

The movements were pretty straightforward, but when I tried to mimic them, I felt stiff and awkward. Jackal repeated his instructions. I tried again but still didn't get the rhythm correct, and I stumbled.

"This is not a court trial, Reason. Get the fuck out of your head. You have to just go on pure instinct."

Gritting my teeth, I repeated the actions. He swatted my hands like a fly, and the staff flew out of my hands. He swept me off my feet, and I plopped hard on the ground. I scrambled to my feet, snatching up the staff, and was now mad as hell.

He snapped out the moves—first slow and then faster. When I was finished, I was sweaty but really pumped. I felt a surge of adrenaline run through my blood. The moves felt right, like I had been doing them for years.

Jackal picked up another staff before walking over to me. "That was a good job for a newbie. But let's see how you do against me."

Without pause, Jackal and I bowed to each other. Then he menacingly circled me, sizing me up. I warily watched him as we circled each other, waiting for an opening. He gave me a bored stare and yawned.

I lunged forward with my staff aimed at his chest. He swiftly stepped back, sneering, as he swung his staff. He smiled deviously when it grazed my arm, drawing blood. But I didn't flinch. Instead, I swung my staff with all my might, catching him on the side of his chest.

He jumped back with a look of utter surprise. His face tightened with anger as he circled around my back, expertly pulling me into his chest, barely pressing his staff under my chin. I knew he was holding back, playing with my head.

"See, this would be a kill move, vampire," he whispered in my ear. "That means no coming back. Do you give up?"

"No," I gritted out.

"Come on, Princess. Just let your daddy's enforcers handle all the fighting. No need to get your hands dirty. Go live in your perfect world with your handpicked consort. Besides, you're not tough enough to fight for yourself, hybrid."

His harsh words cut me to the core. This was more than just sparring. He was punishing me for rebuffing him last night.

Distracted momentarily, I dropped my staff.

He caught my arms, tightly wrapping them across my chest. I was now totally trapped against his body. And the more I squirmed, the tauter his grip became.

"Now you're just making silly mistakes. Give the fuck up," he spit nastily in my ear.

"No."

I was crazy mad now. He was baiting me, and I was going to have none of it. I raised my leg and viciously back-kicked him in his calf, taking great satisfaction when he loosened his grip and stepped back. I snatched my staff, scrambled across the floor, and got into warrior stance.

"I'm not giving up, asshole," I responded with a heavy breath.

I swung my leg, kicking him really hard in his thigh, and he howled with pain as he backed away. I shocked him by stepping forward, and my left leg snaked around him, catching him behind the knee and bringing him down. I gasped when he snatched me and flipped me over, sending me sprawling and then rolling underneath him on the floor.

I was flattened out as he balanced himself on his elbows, keeping his weight off me. I found it hard to breathe as I peered into his green eyes while sweat glistened on his forehead.

"Give up, Reason. I have nothing left to give you or any woman."

I froze. Tears pricked behind my eyelids. I couldn't speak or glance away from him. Then everything changed when I saw the wave of emotions shift in his eyes—sadness, fury, and then coldness.

"You and I know I'm not just any woman. I'm more, and if you can't see that, then you're a fucking coward." I roughly pushed at him. "Now get the hell off me, doggy."

"You know what dogs like to do? Lick and bite." He leaned down, licking my bottom lip before nipping it.

"Shit. Why don't you two get a damn room?" Rip snapped. "I'm out of here."

I heard his retreating footsteps and the elevator open and close.

Despite the fact that Jackal tasted like coffee and mint, essentially delicious, I wasn't going to fall for his shit. "Get off," I gritted out.

He rolled over, allowing me to get to my feet as I grabbed my staff. In a crazy blur, he was on his feet, circling me with a lazy grin. I took the opening, swinging around to deliver a round-house kick to his chest. He expertly used his staff, swiping me off my feet, causing me to flip hard onto the floor. The air was completely knocked from my body. I actually thought I saw stars.

Jackal stood over me with an icy smile on his face and offered me a hand. "Had enough?"

I slapped his hand away. "Hell no." I scrambled to my feet.

His strange gold-rimmed green eyes narrowed. "Okay. Let's go, and this time, watch your breathing."

I threw aside the staff, and he did the same. He stepped backward, standing at his full height, flexing his unbelievably cut, athletic frame.

Well then, let the ass-kicking commence. His ass, not mine.

In the blink of an eye, I launched myself at him like a

deranged reality show cast member, handspringing off the floor and unmercifully kicking him in the chest. He didn't even flinch, but there was a twinkle of admiration in his eyes.

The shifter actually respected my effort, or he got off on pain; both possibilities made the apex of my thighs flutter with excitement.

"Good, but not good enough." He grabbed my arm and pivoted before softly planting a foot into my ribcage, catching me totally unaware. "You're not concentrating, Reason."

Now I was annoyed. "Oh, I'll show you not concentrating." I unleashed another wicked kick, which embarrassingly grazed his chest like a love tap.

"What the fuck was that, vampire? If you're going to kick me, then make me feel the impact in my damn bones." His lips curled up into an honest-to-goodness bad-boy smile. "Bring it... and next time, throw your body into your punches and kicks, pampered princess."

My eyes narrowed. *Pampered?*

My fists clenched and unclenched before I stepped forward in a calculated attack. Jackal didn't go easy on me as we both started going at it with a flurry of kicks, blocks, and punches.

I smiled triumphantly when I somehow got him into a choke hold. My chest pressed against his back with my calves burning from the effort of staying on my toes, given my height disadvantage. I was so close to doing a victory dance when he twisted out of my hold, throwing me over his shoulder like a sack of potatoes, and I landed on the mat with a thump.

Shit, this is going to hurt like hell tomorrow.

Adding insult to injury, he stood over me, glaring. "Stay down, Reason."

"Hell no."

He beckoned me forward with one finger. "Okay. Come to Daddy," he taunted.

"Oh, I got your daddy."

Pissed, I got to my feet and launched myself at him with a

series of kicks that would have made a martial arts master proud. With a back kick, he went sailing to the mat, landing on his back.

"Damn." He laughed huskily. "You fighting like a hellcat is so fucking hot. I'm harder than a rock right now."

I seductively licked my bottom lip before taking a step closer, my body standing alongside his prone body. "Oh, I see. My shifter is a sucker for pain and likes it rough."

I pressed my booted heel on his shoulder. His eyes dilated, which totally turned me on.

I'm so fucked up in the head.

"Very rough." His lips curled up into a beautiful smile.

"Well, I reserve rough play for the bedroom, shifter." I winked at him.

"Good to know, darling." He grabbed my calf and easily yanked my body down, causing my ass to hit the mat with a thud.

"Ouch," I complained.

"Oh, stop whining." He sat up and eased me forward, practically pulling me onto his lap with my legs indecently wide open. He wrapped his thick fingers around my thighs and began kneading the sore muscles.

I groaned aloud, almost drooling, as my aching muscles began loosening. "Damn, you have magic fingers. You must make the ladies happy." My eyelids slid closed.

"Is that your polite way of calling me a manwhore?" He inched up the material of my yoga pants. The warmth of his fingers against the skin on my leg made me shiver with anticipation.

I shrugged. "I just call it like I see it, shifter."

"Well, just so we're clear, I'm a one-woman man," he replied huskily.

My eyes popped open as I jerked my leg away. "You cocky fucker. Do you honestly think, with a half-assed massage and a couple sexy words, that I would strip naked, point to my cunt, and tell you to have at it?"

His eyes narrowed.

"Oh no, shifter. I'm not that easy." After last night, I had closed up my emotional walls. "You want me? Well, welcome to my world of sexual angst and lots of cold showers." I smiled... too sweetly. "We're done here."

His mouth fell open and then closed. "You can't be serious."

Deftly, I rose to my feet. "I'm as serious as a heart attack." Turning on my heel, I muttered, "See you around, shifter," before sauntering away and not sparing him a glance.

"Damn, vampire. I hate to see you leave, but I love to watch you walk away." His gravelly voice sent vibrations of lust throughout my body.

I glanced at him over my shoulder. Jackal smiled, and my heart skipped a beat. The man was beyond handsome when he smiled. But I refused to cave in to my body's lust. I sighed with relief when the empty elevator was already waiting. Stepping in, I pasted on a smile before turning to face him.

Jabbing the first-floor button impatiently, the last thing I saw was his frustrated expression before the door slid closed.

REASON

Idiot, idiot, idiot, I chanted over and over while punching in the elevator security code to Dad's penthouse. The door shut, and I sagged against the railing, recounting Dad's text.

Reason. Get to the penthouse. Now!

Does he know I gave Jackal my blood?

My nerves were a complete mess after just getting a call from Jackal. Soar had finally completed his assessment, and the massive amount of information the hackers had stolen did include Redemption's surveillance data.

Shit, I am so fucked right now.

Maybe I should just fess up and tell Dad what I did. Honesty had to count for something, right?

Who am I kidding? Dad wouldn't give a shit if I threw myself at his feet and begged for mercy and forgiveness. In his eyes, vampire law was vampire law, and he was a stickler for upholding it even if it meant the death of his only child.

A bead of sweat trickled between my breasts as the elevator stopped and the door opened. As I stepped into the hallway with my heart racing, the panic started to take hold.

I yelped when Stefan appeared before me. The fucking vampire was like a ninja.

"Good morning, milady," he greeted.

"What did I tell you about sneaking up on me?" I snapped. "Don't do it."

I eyed Stefan—blond, handsome, and Dad's newly appointed second-in-command—as he gave me a sly grin. And as fucking usual, he was leering like he wanted to slam me to the floor and fuck me into submission.

He bowed his head. "I apologize, milady." His words contradicted his arrogant smirk.

"Go away, Stefan."

I stepped around him, but he followed me into the dining room—the lair of my executioner. My eyes zeroed in on Dad, who was sitting in the dark room at the head of the table, reading a newspaper, with a glass of blood within reach of his fingertips.

"Good morning, Dad," I greeted.

He didn't respond. He was giving me the silent treatment, which meant he was really pissed. I took a seat in the chair to the right of him.

Carmen, his personal chef, strolled out with a cup of espresso and a plate with a fluffy, freshly made chocolate-covered croissant. "There she is. Right on time."

"Thanks, Carmen." I smiled at her warmly when she placed the items before me.

"Anytime." She kissed my cheek before nodding in Dad's direction. "What did you do this time? I haven't seen him this angry since the time you were in high school and decided to shave off your hair, demanding to be emancipated from the tyrannical reign of the bloodthirsty Orlov coven."

I shrugged. "No clue what I did to piss off the great Oskar Orlov."

She clucked her tongue before bustling back into the kitchen.

Dad was still silent with no facial expression while continuing to read. Silence was golden in my book... especially when it came to his wrath. When I was younger, I would only last fifteen minutes under the weight of his silence. Now, not so much. Normally, I didn't give a shit. But today, I was anxious as hell.

I took a huge bite out of my croissant, watching and waiting for him to say something. "Well?" I sipped my espresso, boldly eyeing him. "You summoned me here to reprimand me for something. So let your wrath commence."

Nothing.

Obviously, this didn't have to do with me giving blood to Jackal, or Dad would have been frothing at the mouth with rage.

Yes. Crisis averted.

"Okay. Good-bye, Dad," I grumbled before pushing away my plate. "I've got things to do today." I started to get up. "I'll see you tonight at the gala."

He slowly folded his newspaper. "Ass back in the seat, Reason," he demanded without emotion. Leaning back in his chair, he eyed me. "I heard you were at Angels last night."

I blinked, relieved I'd dodged the Blood Rite bullet.

"And I heard you sent a group of rogue vampires to kill Jackal." I arched a brow. "Do you care to tell me why?"

"I don't answer to you, Reason." He angled his face in a silent warning.

"Then I don't answer to you, Dad." I pressed my palms against the table with my chest heaving. "We had a deal. I agreed to marry that asshole." I jabbed a finger at Stefan. "You agreed to help Ryker and his pack find Light. Nothing in that arrangement talked about you killing off Ryker and his pack."

"Ryker and his pack are just casualties of war. Their deaths will mean nothing once the dust settles." He kept his tone conversational and took a sip from his glass of blood.

I threw my hands up in the air. "I can't do this shit. The wedding is off."

"Is that so?" His eyes were now a mixture of blue and gold, an indication that he was fucking mad.

I didn't flinch. "Do you really want to air our dirty laundry in front of him?" I glared at Stefan, the live statue.

"Stefan, leave," Dad ordered.

Stefan nodded and exited.

Dad tilted his head and studied me. "Because you have proven you are incapable of making sound decisions, I've assigned Stefan as your personal guard."

"No, thank you. I don't need him insinuating himself further into my life."

He banged on the table. "Reason, enough. Stefan is now your guard."

I had no intention of caving on this issue. "You and I have an agreement. I do my duty as Princess Orlov, and you stay the hell out of my personal life." I pursed my lips. "Now, if you want to renegotiate the terms of our agreement, then that's fine with me. But keep in mind, I will walk away from bullshit events like tonight's vampire gala." I tapped my fingers against the table. "So... make your choice."

Dad's cold gaze fixed on me. "I will tolerate many things from you, but there is one thing that will not stand—you shirking your duties as the princess of this coven."

My brows furrowed. "What the hell do you want from me, Dad? I refuse to spend the rest of my life with a fake smile on my face, pretending those backstabbing coven members actually respect my position and me. Just accept they will never respect me in the same way they respect you."

"They don't respect me. They fear me. There's a fucking difference. For that matter, if you would spend more time with your family, then you would understand the coven dynamics, but instead, you prefer to pretend your coven doesn't exist."

"Family?" I scoffed. "They hate me."

"They don't understand you. You don't make it easy by distancing yourself from them and our way of life. Marrying Stefan will change their perspective."

"I'm not marrying Stefan." That was not going to happen

ever, especially now that I knew Dad had no intention of helping Ryker get Light back.

"You will marry him or face the ramifications."

My body stiffened. "He's possessive. Crazy. Volatile. And a killer."

"All traits that make him an ideal consort. He'll protect you with his life. What else do you want, Reason?"

"Happiness, love, chemistry," I answered. "A man I don't have the burning urge to shank every time I see him." *And a man who makes my core wet and respects me as his equal.*

"What does love have to do with taking him as your husband? As the princess of this coven, you are supposed to do two things in life—find a suitable consort and preserve the Orlov bloodline by having vampire babies."

The coldness of his logic should have made me cringe, but I was immune. Dad had been pounding that mantra into my head since I turned eighteen.

"You mean hybrid babies," I retorted.

"I don't care if they're hybrid. Just have them." His eyes narrowed, and his jaw tightened.

It wasn't the proudest moment in my life when I'd agreed to marry Stefan, essentially bartering my life and body in exchange for Dad's help finding Light. *But what did it say about him as a father that he'd allowed me to?* It said, in big neon lights, that my happiness didn't mean crap to him. The continuation of the Orlov bloodline and coven meant more. Always did and always would.

But the burning question that made my gut twist with angst is, whom would Dad choose if push came to shove? The coven or me?

"I'm not going to be able to appease you on this, Dad."

"Stefan has pledged to protect your life with his. In return, you must simply pledge your life to him as his wife and consort. Just do your duty—marry Stefan and preserve our family bloodline."

Frankly, I was exhausted from the never-ending duties

heaped upon me as the daughter of Oskar Orlov, the reigning leader of the Orlov coven and the most feared and powerful vampire in the Northeast.

Unfortunately, Dad didn't give a shit about my opinion on the matter.

His brows furrowed as he grabbed his glass of blood, chugging it like a desperate man.

"What's really going on, Dad?"

"Nothing you need to worry about."

"Dad, talk to me." I reached across the table, grabbing his hand. "You can't continue to shelter me from the real world."

"It's nothing, Reason."

Bullshit! He's hiding something.

"Nothing?" I snorted. "So this has absolutely nothing to do with the war looming between the Others?" I arched a brow.

"Reason," he growled warningly.

"No, Dad, I'm not backing off. You sent rogue assassins to kill Jackal. What were you thinking?" I paused, waiting for him to say something, but he didn't. "You can't continue to shelter me," I repeated. "I will not sit in the ivory tower that you built while a war brews around me." My body trembled with rage. I was exhausted by the fact that he continued to treat me like some fragile doll that would shatter at the mere thought of danger. "I'm tougher than you think, Dad."

He unblinkingly stared at me. "I can't ensure your safety anymore. Not with you running around unprotected."

"No one will mess with me, Dad. Others are terrified of you."

"The Shadows are not, and they're playing by a different set of rules."

"Then help Ryker find Light and take down the Shadows," I pleaded.

"That's shifter business. I have to protect my own."

My mouth flopped open. "How can you say that? Light is like family. We grew up together. Shifter, witch, vampire—it doesn't make a damn difference. The Shadows do not discriminate. They want to wipe *all* Others off the face of the earth."

"I will deal with the Shadows but on my own terms. You might not like my decisions, but I make them because I love you."

"I've never doubted that you love me, Dad."

His eyes narrowed to slits. "Then understand these are dangerous times. The permanent truce Ryker desires will not happen now that the vampires and shifters distrust each other's motives. To make matters worse, our coven is not untouched by the ripple effects of the Shadows presence in New York. I need to ensure your protection if something were to happen to me."

"Dad, you're not going to die."

"I've lived for centuries and seen shit you wouldn't believe. Power is fleeting. I need to guarantee you'll survive when it's all said and done."

"And the Shadows?"

"I have totally different business with the Shadows, and once that's resolved, I'll kill them all."

I frowned. "You can't kill them, Dad. They're Ryker's only lead to finding Light."

"That is none of your concern. Our coven is."

My hands clenched. "I don't care about the coven. I care about saving my friend."

"This is my fault." He sighed. "I thought, with time, you would understand your needs are not important to me. You will be married to Stefan by the end of this month."

His tone ignited my temper.

"Okay, enough! I'm not putting up with this shit anymore."

"And what do you mean by *this shit?*" he asked, his voice low and rough.

I finally threw my arms up in the air with exasperation. "This life. This gilded cage of restrictions and expectations. I will not be pigeonholed as some simpering princess whose sole purpose is to be a fertile vessel for the continuation of the Orlov bloodline. I've busted my ass to prove I'm more. Well, I'm done, and I need you to choose between my happiness and the coven's expectations of me. Right here and right now. Starting with making me a partner at the law firm."

"Have you lost your damn mind? You're simply not ready. In ten more years, our clients will come to accept you, and then—"

I stared at him with my lips pursed in disbelief. "Wrong answer." Steel laced my tone. "I quit," I clipped out while scraping the chair back and easing myself onto my feet.

"Bullshit." His eyes narrowed, and his nostrils flared. "You can't just up and quit."

"I just did," I delivered between clenched teeth before storming out without a backward glance.

✤ 12 ✤

REASON

I STRODE out of my townhouse, feeling refreshed after a long nap. After leaving Dad's penthouse, I had gone home and, for the first time in years, enjoyed a day off. There was no worrying about clients, the firm, or how many cases I had to review. Nope. It was just me, lazing around my house, relishing just being still... for once.

It was like a weight had been lifted after I uttered the words, "I quit."

Now I was free to forge my own way. I didn't worry about tomorrow or what was next. I knew the answer would come... eventually.

I heard my cell ringing in my clutch, and I knew who it was before even looking at it. Dad. He had been calling all day, and I had been ignoring him. Frankly, there was nothing else for us to talk about. I still loved him, but our relationship would never be the same. After I completed my obligations tonight, there would be no more vampire soirees or coven events. I was done with that life. And I was done with him.

I smiled at Dad's newest and youngest enforcer, Declan. He was waiting patiently, leaning against a sleek black luxury SUV.

"I apologize for the delay," I uttered before a yawn escaped from my lips. "But the time just got away from me."

"Good evening, milady. No apologies needed." He pushed away, tilting his head toward me. "You look lovely, as usual." He glanced at me from head to toe with an appreciative gleam in his eyes while opening the back door.

I smiled impishly. "Thank you, Declan," I replied, handing him my small designer luggage bag and then maneuvering my gown into the limo. "So you drew the short straw and got stuck on this detail, huh?" I asked while fastening my seat belt.

"Yep, as fucking usual." He grinned before shutting the door. He scampered around to the trunk to stow my bag before walking over to the driver's side, sliding in and facing me. "But I don't mind because I get to hang out with the hottest vampire in Manhattan," he offered, smiling at me.

I winked. "Damn, if you were a couple years older, I'd make you mine, vampire."

I loved messing with Declan. As the youngest enforcer, he tended to get pushed around by the other members of the team, but I knew he was the smartest one out of the bunch. He just needed his confidence boosted a bit so he could survive moving up the ranks.

"Thank you, BLC." He blushed bright red before turning around. Declan fastened his seat belt before twisting the key and revving the engine.

"Wait... what's BLC?" I asked.

"Bad Luck Charm. The new nickname the senior enforcers gave you today."

I frowned. "Why?"

"Oh, let me count the ways, milady. In the span of a week, you've managed to get three enforcers seriously injured." He smoothly pulled into Manhattan traffic before zipping in and out of the snarl of taxicabs and buses.

"Who the hell are the injured enforcers?"

"Your father was really pissed you gave them, your newly

assigned enforcers, the slip today. So as punishment for their incompetence, he broke their arms and legs."

I gasped. "Shit. My bad."

"Don't worry about it. They'll heal eventually." He chuckled. "Don't tell him I said so, but your father is on a wild tear. All the enforcers are scared as shit of getting on his bad side. So don't even think about doing anything crazy, like carjacking me and driving off to Mexico. I'm young and fragile, and I wouldn't live through your father ripping my heart out."

"You're a vampire. You'd survive," I grumbled under my breath while frowning at the New York City gridlock. I knew Dad had a wicked temper, but breaking body parts was a new low.

Pensive, I clasped my hands together while staring through the window, watching Declan smoothly drive through traffic. "So, Declan, how many hours to get to the château?"

"In this traffic? Not long."

My thoughts veered to tonight's event. I wasn't exactly excited to be attending Dad's extravagant gala. I could barely tolerate being in the company of the coven, and tonight would be a hundred times worse. Vampire kings and queens from all regions would be gathered tonight in celebration of their annual Vampire Leadership Strategy Retreat.

Dad had pulled out all the stops by renting a lavish château and hiring an event planner to plot tonight's extravaganza and all of this weekend's events. It would also be intense with all that power in one room, jockeying for alliances with the most ruthless leader in the Northeast—Dad.

I jumped, startled, when Declan announced, "We're here."

Yawning, I glanced at the fortress-like château situated in the flat saddle of a forest partway up the mountain, next to a lake. It was impressive. The property was surrounded by high stone walls, and the stately grounds were bathed in floodlights and patrolled by armed guards with dogs.

The driveway was filled with cars. We slowed and were in line to be dropped off. Declan pulled up to the venue and stopped. He got out of the vehicle, opened the door, and reached for me.

I took a deep breath and hesitated. "Well, all righty. Time to make tonight my bitch," I grumbled.

"I'll drive around back and bring your luggage inside. Have a good time, milady."

Declan smiled at me, and I grabbed his hand.

"Thanks, Declan," I stated as I stepped out.

Swaying away, I schooled my face into my I-don't-give-a-shit facade. Even after growing up under the coven's scrutiny, I wasn't as comfortable with socializing with them, so I had to go somewhere else in my mind and pretend I was a confident person in front of a horde of bloodthirsty, power-hungry vampires mixed with a smattering of shifters.

The hem of my dress swirled around my ankles as my stilettos clicked against the pavement. I lifted my gown's train as I ascended the red-carpeted staircase.

Tonight's gala was a tribute to all the rich, elite vampires congregated at the venue. It was Dad's attempt at being magnanimous in the eyes of vampires. But the reality was even worse. Under the veil of camaraderie, he was lulling them into a false sense of security that he actually gave a shit about uniting the vampires. He didn't; he wanted their territories. His motto was, *Keep your friends close and your enemies closer.*

I bypassed the guests that were handing over their invitations for inspection while other guests waited patiently as a white-gloved security staffer politely scanned their bodies with a handheld metal detector. Two of Dad's enforcers stood before massive carved wooden doors, wearing smart business attire and a clear secret-service earpiece. When I approached, they bowed, opened the doors, and scurried out of the way.

I surveyed the scene upon entering the château. The blaring music grated against my frayed nerves. The gala was in full swing, reminding me of how much I truly hated these events.

My mouth tightened at the sound of laughter floating through the air. "Yes, laugh it up. No need to worry about the Shadows hunting down vampires and shifters like animals," I grumbled. "Just toast it up, vampire-style, and ignore our new reality." I incredulously shook my head.

Despite living my whole life around vampires, I still didn't understand their frivolity, given our precarious situation.

A giant chandelier made from hundreds of crimson roses conspicuously hung above, and the main staircase was surrounded by walls covered with pristine white roses. At the top of the staircase, Dad regally stood and greeted arriving guests.

Grabbing my gown's train, I slowly made my way up the stairs. Tonight, I'd made sure to go all out with my appearance. My crystal-embellished nude illusion dress boasted both swirling embroidery and large three-dimensional silver floral appliqués down the bodice and around the hemline of the design. On my head, I wore a matching silver headdress with the same crystal adornments and floral accents. For makeup, I'd created a look just as bold as the dress with thick arched brows, rust eye shadow on my lids, and a berry pout. My hairstyle was a side-swept chignon to show off my tattoo-covered back. I always got a kick out of showing my tattoos because Dad hated them so much.

I froze when I felt something brush against my ass. Whirling around so fast, I almost stumbled down the stairs before firm hands gripped and steadied me. They were Stefan's. The idiot was holding on to me with a fucking idiot look on his face.

He smiled while eyeing the deep-V neckline plunging down to my belly button. "Milady." He bowed his head.

I pulled away from him, stepping securely onto the landing. "Did you just touch my ass?" I snapped, pointing in his face.

"I couldn't help myself. Damn, you are so tempting."

He stepped closer, spreading his hand across my hip. I promptly knocked it off.

I refused to let him intimidate me. With my chin tilted at a stubborn angle, I held my ground. "Touch me again, and I will fuck you up. I don't care who's watching, including my dad," I said, my voice flat.

He held his hands up in front of him in fake surrender. "Whoa. Slow down, kitten." He laughed.

I was done with his stupid ass. "Why are you stalking me, Stefan?"

"Stalking? Hardly. I'm just protecting what's mine"—he licked his lips and studied me—"and counting the days until I get you in my bed to seal the deal." He grinned like he'd won the fucking lottery. Grabbing my hand, he brought it up to his lips, gently kissing it. His hard lips were frigid against my skin.

I yanked my hand away, barely suppressing the urge to wipe it on my gown to remove any trace of his touch.

"We're not getting married... ever," I stated with a sneer.

His lips twitched into a mockery of a smile. "The marriage will happen, Reason. One way or another. And if I have to drag you to the altar, kicking and screaming, so be it." He reached down, tracing a finger against my shoulder. "I've killed countless men to prove my worthiness to your father. I've kissed that fucker's shoes to show my humbleness, and I'll be damned if I let you part your fucking legs for that shifter, Jackal."

My mouth dropped open and then closed.

"Yes, Reason. I know about you and him. I saw you at Angels, panting and salivating over him like a bitch in heat. But remember this; you are mine, and if I catch that dog sniffing around you again, I will fucking kill him."

I scrunched up my nose. He was truly a worthless piece of shit.

"You mean you'll *try* to kill him. Jackal is no easy win, Stefan. So if you think you can threaten me and I'll roll over and concede, you have another damn thing coming. And just so we're clear, I wouldn't fuck you even if you had a thousand-dollar bill stuck to your limp cock."

His smile slipped. "Liar," he accused. "I see the way you stare at me when you think I'm not looking."

I scrutinized him as if he'd lost his mind. *The dude is fucking delusional.*

I balled up my fist, stepping toward him. "That's a look of disgust. Get a damn clue, Stefan."

"You're fighting a battle you can't win, Reason. Your father and I have made the decision."

I felt Dad's disapproving stare. Knowing him, he'd been watching my encounter with Stefan, and he was none too pleased. I caught Dad's eye. His mouth was set in a firm line. Raw power emanated from his essence as his gaze slid away from me to dissect everyone around him.

"We will be married," Stefan spit. "It's up to you if you want to make it easy or difficult. You choose."

I eyed him. "I choose difficult." My nostrils flared. "Now fuck off." I smiled icily.

Fury twisted Stefan's face. "This is far from over, Reason." His dark tone rang with deadly promise.

"It is for me," I hissed before turning on my heel, walking across the landing and up the stairs with my head held high.

The top of the staircase opened to a huge space. My eyes flickered through the room. The stunning venue had been transformed for the occasion with light-gray sofas and flowers placed throughout. It was amazing and hard to take in the splendor all at once. My eyes paused on Vivica and a woman I didn't recognize. They were huddled together, whispering, while giving the guests sly glances.

Dad advanced forward and inclined his head. "You're late," he remarked while adjusting his bow tie.

I grudgingly had to admit he looked ultra sharp in his black tuxedo with a white silk cummerbund.

My lips pursed. "I'm not in the mood to argue tonight. Just be happy I came to this circus."

We faced off. The tension between us was so thick I could cut it with a knife.

Dad's eyes narrowed, displeasure turning down the corners of his mouth. He bit out, "I saw you and Stefan talking. Did you two work out your differences? We have a wedding to plan."

Dad was like a dog with a bone.

Why can't he let this consort thing go?

Rage coursed through my veins. I was his flesh and blood, and he'd offered me up to Stefan like a sacrificial lamb. It burned me to the core that I was nothing but a pawn to him.

"Wedding? I quit the job that I'd busted my ass at for years to prove I deserved it, and all you can talk about is me getting married?" I shook my head in disbelief. "I'm so done. After tonight, I want nothing to do with you or the coven."

"Do you actually think I will allow you to just walk away?" He laughed. "I am your creator. Everything you have is because of me."

I flinched as if he'd physically slapped me. "If that were true, I would be an evil, soulless monster... like you. But I'm not. I don't need you anymore. My life is my own."

"You, my beautiful daughter, are a hybrid. You won't last a day without my protection. Remember that."

One of his enforcers walked up to him. "Excuse me, Sire, but there's an emergency." He eyed me before leaning toward Dad's ear and whispering quietly.

"Shit." Dad's body tightened, and then his eyes locked onto me like magnets. "Reason, I have business to attend to. We'll continue our conversation later."

"No, we won't," I retorted. "Now go do what you do best. Tend to the needs of your beloved coven and leave me the hell alone."

His eyes went cold before he turned away, promptly dismissing me to walk with his enforcer. My stomach cramped with angst from our confrontation. Emotionally and physically, the tension between us was tearing me apart.

Over the years, I'd looked the other way, pretending not to see all the violent, destructive things he'd done in the quest for power and territory. Now the blinders had been ripped off. And for the first time in my life, I saw him for the man he truly was—dark, uncaring, manipulative, and controlling.

I was startled out of my thoughts by Vivica's voice. "Reason, get your gorgeous ass over here."

I made a beeline toward her.

Once I was there, Vivica kissed my cheek before saying, "Go ahead. Tell me how hot I look." She twirled around, flaunting her slim figure in the super-sexy design, which showed a whole lot of cleavage, courtesy of its plunging neckline. Vivica paired the show-stopping frock with gold ankle-strap heels and kept her hair stick straight for a dramatic flair.

"Vivica, as usual, you're smoking hot." I winked at her. "But what are you doing here? You're the last person I expected to see."

She hated vampire-attended affairs with a purple passion and normally stayed clear of them. It was an odd relationship, given the fact she was very influential and powerful within the vampire and Others community.

"I know how you hate coming to these events, so I had to come and keep you company." She looped an arm through mine.

We walked toward the thick of the gala patrons milling around. Music blared from the band onstage. Vampires danced and mingled in the ballroom. Some of them were gathered in the corners, drinking blood from live human donors.

I side-eyed her. "What are you really doing here?"

She sighed. "Your dad told me about your disagreement."

"So I guess you're going to tell me I made a big mistake by quitting." It was a statement, not a question.

"Guess again. Frankly, I'm fucking proud of you. It's about time you stood up to Oskar."

I glanced at her with shock. "Really?"

She nodded. "Oskar and I have been friends for years. I respect him for his strength and leadership, but he's never been the sharpest pencil when it comes to you. He just doesn't get it. Brute force will never work with you. He means well, but I warned him about his overprotectiveness. I told him it was unwise and foolish to believe, because you are a hybrid, he has to cover you up in bubble wrap." She smiled. "You, my beautiful Reason, are a fighter. Just like me."

"Thank you," I whispered, touched.

"Think nothing of it. I'll always have your back. Besides, this party is wonderfully fun. You don't know how much I enjoy making these kings and queens squirm from my mere presence. The whole lot of them are pretentious, uptight pricks." Vivica practically glided across the floor. "I bet you didn't know I used to work for Credence Other Corporation as an escort," she stated matter-of-factly.

"No, I didn't." Even as the attorney for the Credence Other Corporation—secretly New York's most sought-after Others escort service—there was still so much I didn't know about their business and clients.

"I was one of their best girls, if I do say so myself. But this was way before you were born." Her eyes momentarily darted around. "See how the women are clutching their men for dear life?"

I nodded.

"That's because most of the men in this room were my clients." She snickered. "And I had their husbands ready to leave them with just four words uttered from me. *Yes, I'll marry you.* Back then, I was really rough around the edges when the Credence family took me in and gave me a home and life direction." She sighed. "I went from a distrustful, resentful vamp who thought the world was out to get her to a woman who was ready to embrace life. When I found my mates, it was time to quit.

Trust me when I say life is about taking chances and leaving the past behind."

I studied her. "What are you really trying to tell me, Vivica?"

"That men make mistakes. They say and do fucked-up things in haste... and pain. But that shifter of yours... Jackal, will come to see that a jewel as precious as you is worth the fight."

I suspiciously eyed her. "How did you—"

"I did some checking. I had to make sure he would give you the love and respect you deserved." She winked. "And I'm confident he's up to the task, darling. You just have to give him the chance to prove it."

I blinked back the emotions, letting her words sink in.

We strolled amiably among the glittering and star-studded rich men and women. I snagged a canapé from the passing waiter. Vampires preened for the photographer floating through the crowd. Shrewdly, Dad had ensured that only the most powerful vampires were invited.

Attending enough of these events had taught me how to move in a roomful of vultures. Men's eyes followed me with blatant interest, and their dates tensely clutched onto them while their gazes shot daggers at me. It was a calculated fashion risk when I'd decided to wear the dramatic see-through, crystal-studded couture gown tonight. The sheer fabric gave a cheeky peek at my bum as we sliced through the guests.

Reaching the venue's midpoint, I glanced across the room, only to see Jackal holding court with Rip by the bar. My eyes locked with Jackal's, and then the crowd shifted, cutting off our view of each other.

"Damn. Shit just got real," I muttered under my breath.

The throng moved again. Jackal was checking me out with unveiled interest.

I tried to calm my beating heart, but to no avail. Biting my bottom lip, I drank him in. Jesus, he was sexy. If you looked *fuckable* up in the dictionary, Jackal's name would be right there next to it. He sizzled in a shawl-collared tuxedo paired with a crisp tailored white shirt, black silk bow tie, and black leather shoes. Rip was flawless in a black tuxedo. They were masculinity at its finest.

Jackal's eyes flashed as he arched his eyebrow at me. I stopped and turned so I was facing Vivica and my back was toward Jackal.

Vivica curiously peered at me. "What's up?"

"Don't look. Jackal's by the bar," I hissed.

Of course, she did the exact opposite of what I'd asked and stared boldly in his direction.

I wanted to choke her. "Really? What part of *don't look* was unclear?"

Staring over my shoulder, Vivica whispered loudly, "I know he's here. I invited him."

"Why?"

"Because I'm a sucker for happy endings." She grinned. "Now kick off your stilettos and dash across the room and into his waiting arms."

I blinked and then blinked again. The woman was certifiably insane.

I turned back around, frowning at him. I'd be damned if I acknowledged the way my nether lips pulsed under his scrutiny. Damn, but braving a roomful of bloodthirsty pariahs just to see me... well, that was kind of hot.

He appeared hard, domineering, and in control. The disdain in his eyes as he scowled at the spoiled rich patrons said he didn't like them. He barely tolerated them. At least he and I had that much in common. He just didn't fit into their world, despite his ultra-expensive suit and shoes.

"A shifter at a vampire soirée? He's crazy," I muttered.

"You mean crazy hot." She wiggled her eyebrows. "Shit, I'd let him cuff me and spank me, and I'd beg him to allow me to call him Sir."

An elderly woman watched Vivica with contempt.

Vivica eyed her right back. "Move along, lady, before I spill the beans about all the dirty, filthy things your husband asked me to do to him behind closed doors. Code word, *golden showers*."

I slapped my hands over my mouth to stop the laughter. "I can see you're planning on making trouble tonight."

"What's new? Besides, you need a little trouble in your life." She looped her arm through mine and pulled. "We must go over and bask in your shifter's and his sidekick's hotness."

I didn't budge. "Nope, we're not doing that," I replied simply.

Vivica smiled widely. "Yes, we are." She paused. "But if you want me to make a scene and call them over, I can do that, too. It's your choice, sweetness."

I growled.

Vivica had the finesse of a bull in a china shop. I knew she would take pleasure in making a scene for a multitude of reasons.

"Fine, let's go."

She smugly looked at me. "I knew you'd see it my way." She pulled me through the crowd, toward Jackal and Rip.

Jackal's eyes traveled from the top of my head and down my curvy body. His wolfish stare made me feel like a mouse beneath the ferocious gaze of a cat.

I raised my chin in a gesture of defiance.

"Damn... that's hot," Vivica muttered. "He's checking you out, all marauder-like."

And he *was* checking me out. His smoldering gaze slowly perused my length in a deliberate way. I went breathless, right to the pit of my stomach. I didn't understand how he had the power to make me feel excited, giddy, and turned on all at the same time.

His mouth curved in that secret way that said he knew how much I wanted him.

Dammit. This is not good.

"And what do you expect him to do?" I asked her. "Throw me to the floor and plunder me like a pirate?"

"Why not? Don't pirates like the booty?" She saucily smiled at me, tugging me along.

I wanted to walk in the opposite direction, fleeing from his disturbing heated focus. But Jackal was a beast to prey, and any sign of fear would be my doom and his victory.

Rip said something to him. Jackal nodded before they both stalked away from the bar.

Vivica stopped, incredulously gawking at me. "Where the hell are they going?"

I tried to quash the glimmer of disappointment as I watched them navigate through the crowd and up the winding staircase located at the back of the room.

"Hopefully home!" I exclaimed while grabbing a champagne flute from a passing tray before downing it like water.

"Well, you're no fun," Vivica commented before pouting playfully.

The band abruptly stopped playing music, and Dad's voice boomed from the microphone. I turned around to face the front of the space where Dad was located on the large stage.

"Welcome to our annual Vampire Leadership Strategy Retreat," Dad thundered. "The Orlov coven is honored to be hosting this most important event."

The crowd clapped.

"Tonight's gala is the prelude to a weekend of hard work. Important decisions must be made, and my request for an alliance with the Shadows is one of many."

Some guests cheered, and some mumbled with disapproval.

I choked on my drink. *An alliance with the Shadows?*

"Vivica, what the hell is going on?"

"It's obvious. Your father has totally lost his ever-loving mind," she replied.

Dad cleared his throat before saying, "There's a challenging road ahead for vampires, and the key to our survival is joining the Shadows in the annihilation of our enemy—the shifters."

The guests applauded.

The lights dimmed, and strobe lights flickered.

"What a poignant, wonderful speech," a man's voice bellowed.

The heavy red velvet curtain that cloaked the back of the stage swung open to reveal a well-dressed man. He strode over to stand beside Dad as if he had every right to be there.

I shifted uncomfortably. The defiant gleam in the man's eyes told me he was here to start trouble.

"Who is that?" Vivica whispered.

"I don't know," I replied.

Whoever he was, by the smile on Dad's face, it was a friend, not foe.

Dad nodded at him. "You may address them now."

The man smiled at the curious crowd before saying, "My name is Baptiste Thomas. I am the leader of the Shadows."

Guests gasped with horror.

Holy shit.

This was the man I'd heard about. Light's grandfather, the man responsible for her disappearance.

I pushed through the guests with Vivica by my side.

How dare he come here and flaunt his existence when he has my best friend?

I finally made it to the stage, climbing the stairs with curled fists. My stomach twisted with rage intermixed with angst.

"Where's Light, you bastard?" I demanded, prepared to fuck him up.

Baptiste stared at me. "And there she is... Reason Orlov. Your pampered princess, who is apparently beyond reproach." He glanced back at the guests. "It saddens me to tell you that the vampire covenant has been broken by one of your own." He eyeballed me.

My steps faltered slightly.

Oh shit. No. Just fucking no. He couldn't know.

He winked at me, and then I knew he did. More importantly, my whole world was going to be torn apart in front of my father and every vampire king and queen in the United States.

"Reason? What is he talking about?" Dad demanded.

My legs felt like rubber. My heart raced, as if I'd just run a marathon, and I wished to God that the floor would just swallow me up.

Jesus Christ, I'm so fucked.

From the corner of my eye, I saw Jackal slicing through the crowd toward me, eyes glued on Baptiste.

I shook my head. Jackal stopped in his tracks.

"Dad, I..." I swallowed hard. "I should have told you."

Dad's eyes narrowed. "Told me what?"

"That she gave the shifter named Jack Alagona her blood," Baptiste answered. "Is that not forbidden?" He arched a brow.

The whole room stilled and went deadly quiet.

"Impossible!" Dad answered.

"I have proof." Baptiste held up his cell. "Video footage taken outside of Redemption, catching the princess in the act."

My heart thumped hard in my chest. The Shadows were the hackers, and now Baptiste had the evidence that would put the final nail in my coffin.

Vivica pushed forward, attempting to take the stage. Dad's enforcers blocked her.

"Move," Vivica demanded. "That's my niece, and I do not intend on standing by while you fuckers vilify her."

"Enough!" Dad yelled in Vivica's direction. "This is between me and my daughter." He turned to stare at me. "Reason, is this true? Did you give that filthy shifter your blood?" Dad asked, disbelief clear in his eyes and tone.

My mouth flopped open and closed, like a fish out of water. My pulse raced. This was my worst nightmare, but there was no use in denying what had already been revealed. "Yes. I did it to save Jackal's life."

Dad's eyes were blazing. It was a look of fury I'd never seen on his face toward me before.

"Reason! No!" Jackal yelled while storming toward me.

I held up my hand, halting him. "It is done, Jackal. No more hiding. No more secrets." I'd spent my entire life being worried about what people thought of me. Keeping up an illusion of perfection was exhausting.

I watched as Dad's enforcers swarmed around him and Rip.

"I dare you fuckers to touch me or her," Jackal threatened as he shoved them. "I will fucking kill all of you."

Rip and Jackal were back-to-back when all hell broke loose. The two shifters were fighting against my dad's enforcers. Fists flew. The crowd parted. Guests yelled and screamed in a mad dash to get out of the way of the chaos.

Baptiste eyed me before saying, "What is the penalty for her defiance of your law? Not even the great Orlov's daughter is above punishment. Is that not so?"

"Why are you doing this?" I directed at Baptiste. "Me breaking vampire covenant has nothing to do with you or the Shadows."

"But it does, Princess. I was prepared to take your little secret to the grave. But that was before I discovered the filthy shifter, Ryker, stole my property, Light, with the assistance of your father. No one fucks with what's mine. Now the great vampire king must learn what it feels like to have what's so precious to him snatched away." Baptiste's face was a mask of hate.

His words evoked both joy and fear. Joy that Light had finally been rescued and was safe with her mate, Ryker. And fear because my death was surely imminent.

Dad's face went completely blank, and I knew then, before he even spoke, what he would say and do.

"Kings and Queens," he declared unemotionally, "what say you as the punishment for my daughter's crime?"

They raised their champagne glasses in the air and chanted, "Blood Rite, Blood Rite, Blood Rite."

A muscle twitched beneath Dad's right eye. "Let it be so."

13

REASON

IN TYPICAL VAMPIRE FASHION, the coven wasted no time in ordering the Blood Rite to commence. Shortly after the mayhem and chaos that had ensued after Baptiste announced to the guests that I had given Jackal my blood, I had been whisked away to my château suite and ordered to wait there until the enforcers came to get me for sentencing.

Emotionally, I was numb while I stripped off my gown and jewelry and slipped into a pair of jeans and a T-shirt. Sitting on the edge of the bed, I pulled on a pair of socks and then my combat boots.

Oddly, I wasn't scared about my impending death, and I didn't know why. I should have been shaking in my boots or rolling around on the ground in a hysterical crying fit. But I wasn't. I was cool as a cucumber. I would not go down without a fight. I was an Orlov, and we didn't go quietly into the night.

Getting to my feet, I pulled my hair into a tight ponytail as I paced back and forth with my mind racing, trying to think of a fight strategy to make it out of this Blood Rite alive. The rules were clear. If I was successful in my challenge, my offense against the coven would be forgiven and my life spared. If I lost, I would die. Quickly, my thoughts shifted through all the nuances of the Blood Rite, hoping to find a loophole.

"Okay, think, Reason. First, Dad will ask for someone to do the bidding of the coven. Of course, that will be asshole Stefan. Then Dad will ask whether it will be weapons or hand-to-hand."

Physically, there was no way I could beat Stefan in a hand-to-hand battle, nor did I have enough weapon experience to win that fight.

Damn, I'm going to die.

Whether it was slow or fast, it was going to be a painful death.

～

I WAS MARCHED DOWN THE STAIRS, AND IMMEDIATELY, I noticed, instead of the normal frolicking and celebration that accompanied a Blood Rite, the crowd was somber and vigilant.

The crowd parted as the enforcers brought me to the front of the room where Dad stood on the stage, still wearing his formalwear. I steeled myself for a gaze of hatred, but when my eyes met his, they were neutral. He flicked a glance toward Stefan, who was lining up the heavy swords on the floor.

"Reason Orlov, you have been brought before me for breaking the vampire covenant," Dad declared, never taking his eyes off me for a second. "We take blood. We do not give blood."

I sensed his anger simmering just below the surface.

I swallowed hard and bit my bottom lip to hide the emotion that had it trembling.

He turned to stare at the crowd. "Blood for blood," he clipped out.

The guests held up their glasses. "Blood for blood," they chanted.

Dad's nostrils flared, and every muscle in his body seemed to tense, straining against his suit even more. "Since the man you have forfeited your life for is not here to fight and prove he was worthy of your blood, this presents an unprecedented issue. You have no one to fight on your behalf in the Blood Rite." His jaw clenched as he stared at me, unmoving. "According to the rules, I must ask for volunteers to take his place in combat." He glanced at the crowd. "Will anyone fight for Reason Orlov's life?"

There was utter silence.

"I will fight for my own life." I pinned him with a glare.

I could almost see the tic in the side of Dad's face.

"Impossible. You're a hybrid and therefore no match for anyone in a fight."

Thanks for the vote of confidence, Dad.

I refused to let him intimidate me. With my chin tilted at a stubborn angle, I held my ground. "Try me," I clipped out.

"While I commend your bravery, the idea of you fighting in combat is absurd. It is beyond me why you would throw your life away for a fucking shifter who wasn't man enough to fight for you." Dad shook his head, the look on his face something close to disgust. "Jackal is a coward, and you... you're just fucking reckless. But you are my daughter, and I will do what I must to preserve your life." He shrugged off his jacket and rolled up the sleeves of his crisp white dress shirt to reveal his muscular forearms. "So if no one will fight for your honor, then I'm duty-bound to do so."

There was no doubt in my mind he would win. He was that ruthless. But my heart broke at the irony of this situation. If Dad fought, he would lose control of the coven. It was against covenant law for the leader to interfere with the Blood Rite, and essentially, that was what he was doing by fighting for me.

Tears rolled down my cheeks. This was proof that Dad loved me more than his life and the coven.

There was a loud commotion at the back of the room.

The doors flung open, and Jackal stormed in, looking pissed. In each hand, he held an unconscious man. "I thought I heard my name being mentioned." He dumped the men to the floor like rag dolls. "Sorry I'm late. I had to go through two of your elite enforcers to get here."

A sudden hush rolled over the crowd.

Rip and Vivica brought up the rear.

What are the three of them doing together?

"Reason is mine, my mate, and I'll fight for her life," Jackal declared evenly while barreling through the crowd to stand by my side.

I slid a glance to Dad, who hadn't moved, and then back to Jackal. "Jackal, what are you doing here?" I stared at him with my lips pursed in disbelief.

He reached out and touched the side of my face. "Reason, trust me. Let me do what I do best." He watched me closely, the gleam in his eyes making me feel precious and beautiful.

My heart thumped hard in my chest. "But—"

He placed a finger against my lips. "No buts. I would fight the devil himself for you." He leaned down fast, pressing his lips to mine. He trapped me in place with his hands around my face and deepened the kiss, swiping his tongue into my mouth. He broke the kiss, his eyes dilated, as his breathing became heavy.

I blinked back the tears when the truth finally sank in that, even amid all the chaos, darkness, hatred, and despair, love had found us.

Stefan sputtered, "This is ridiculous. He's not a vampire, so he can't fight for her."

Vivica swayed forward. "According to the rules, he can. He has vampire blood, remember?"

She winked at me, and then I knew. Vivica had schooled Jackal on the rules of the Blood Rite. Now he was fully armed with the requirements to win.

Dad nodded. "So be it." He serenely regarded me. "Reason, come take your place beside me."

I swallowed hard, my pulse picking up a little, as I went to stand by Dad. I was scared to death for Jackal. To have someone so strong and good care for my well-being was fucking over-whelming.

Dad glanced at his row of enforcers. "Who will do the bidding of the coven?"

Stefan stepped forward. "It would be my honor, Sire."

Dad nodded. "Weapons or hand-to-hand?" he asked Jackal.

"Hand-to-hand." Muscular forearms crossed in front of him while he stared pointedly at Stefan.

"Let it be so," Dad pronounced.

"I was hoping it would be you, pretty boy," Jackal spoke in his quiet, rough voice. "Let's go, fucker." He beckoned Stefan with his index finger.

The crowd parted. Stefan and Jackal squared off in the middle of the floor, rearing up to fight. It was a powder keg ready to explode. That was the only way to describe the face-off between Jackal and Stefan.

Jackal dived straight into the fire with Stefan. My heart thumped wildly in my chest at the sight of his canines length-ening past his lips, sharp and dangerous.

Both men brawled back and forth for fifteen straight minutes, pausing only to rile each other up with small taunts. Jackal unloaded on Stefan, dropping him multiple times. Stefan brushed it off and seemed ready to put in some work. Jackal was meticulous and calculating with his strikes. I'd never seen anyone move with such precision and quickness. It was like he antici-pated every move that Stefan would make. A legendary brawl was unfolding before our eyes; it was violent and frantic. Jackal was fighting poetically, forcing Stefan to get a little sloppy.

This was a fight that might never be equaled in terms of pure excitement.

Bloodied, battered, and bruised, they stood in the middle of the floor, every person in the room cheering and applauding. Jackal landed a hook square to Stefan's jaw, stunning him. He capitalized by putting Stefan in a perfect clinch while unloading some of the most brutal knee strikes to his body. When Jackal released the clinch, Stefan fell face-first onto the floor.

Stefan was badly injured, but he got up and sprinted for the heavy swords lying on the floor. He snatched one up. The crowd gasped with outrage. He had broken a rule of the Blood Rite. This was hand-to-hand combat; no weapons were allowed. But before Stefan could even turn around and raise the sword for the kill strike, in a move that was unprecedented, even for a vampire, Jackal ripped Stefan's head from his torso in one swift motion.

Holy shit! I stared at Jackal with pride bubbling in my chest. *He won!*

Jackal turned to glare at Dad. "Are we finished now? Or is there anyone else I need to kill? Because I'm just getting warmed up."

"No," Dad replied. "You are done, shifter."

Jackal winked at me. "Are you ready to go?"

"Hell yeah, shifter."

"Good." He lifted me off the stage before placing me on my feet. "Because you and I have a long, hot, and sweaty night ahead of us before I mark you and finally claim you as mine." He gave me a hard kiss on the lips before pulling back.

"Damn, I'm so hot for you right now," I whispered.

He growled playfully. "Less talking and more walking, vampire." He grabbed my hand, pulling me through the crowd that parted like the Red Sea, making way for us.

"What the hell was that superhuman-warrior thing?" I asked.

"Strange shit has been happening ever since you gave me your blood. It's like some high-octane energy drink. I could anticipate every move that fucker was going to make." He winked at me. "I guess there are some benefits to this vampire-blood thing."

❦ 14 ❦

REASON

As I rode the elevator with Jackal, there was a comfortable silence while he tightly held my hand as if he were afraid to let it go. I bit my lower lip, fighting the urge to cry—not sad tears, but happy ones.

Jackal had confirmed Light was safe and back with her mate. I couldn't believe Dad had had a role to play in getting her back. He had called Ryker and his pack, telling them Baptiste would be at the vampire gala. The pack had a hunch that where Baptiste went, Light wouldn't be very far away. And even though Baptiste had had his henchmen guarding Light in an empty suite at the château, Ryker could sense and locate her through their mating bond.

Now all was right in my world.

The elevator door opened into his apartment, and he ushered me along to his living room. There were so many things I wanted to say, but instead, I just waited for him to break the silence.

A hand circled my nape. The heat of his touch set my skin afire as we stood face to face. I leaned back against his fingers, aching for more.

"Reason, I know I acted like an asshole, but it was just hard for me to—"

I touched my fingers to his lips, silencing him. "You don't have to say it."

He kissed my fingers one by one before removing them from his lips. "I do have to say this. I was angry with myself and too concerned with beating myself up because, after all these years, I still held myself accountable for Josie's death. I spent so many years feeling guilty. She died because of me." He heaved a sigh. "And then you came along when I thought I would live my life alone. I felt guilty that I actually saw a glimmer of a happy life without her. A life with you and me." He swallowed hard. "Frankly, the way you make me feel scares the shit out of me."

"Why?"

"Because it's been so long since I've wanted a woman so much... and not just in my bed, but also in my heart." He caressed my back. "My inner wolf wanted you on sight. It was the man who refused to accept the fact that what we had was so deep it touched my mind and soul. But the truth of the matter is I'm so fucking afraid that fate is playing with me, giving me hope that I have another chance at love again, only to snatch you away."

My breath caught in my throat as I blinked hard. "Jackal, nothing real can be threatened if you believe our connection is genuine. I want you in my life and bed forever, but last night, you hurt me and made me feel like shit when you walked away from me." I wasn't too proud to reveal his rebuff had made me feel worthless. "But I promise you if you do that shit again, turn your back on me when the going gets rough, I will be done with you."

He let his hand slip down my body to my hip. Leaning in, he kissed my throat and then bit the same spot. "Reason, please, forgive me?" he asked huskily. "I swear, every day of my life, I'll do everything I can to prove myself worthy of you." He rubbed his nose against my neck before his head snapped up.

It filled me with relief that he realized what we had was stronger than his pride.

"You'd better." I touched his face. "I've always known you are the man for me."

I grabbed his face. He winced.

"Damn, I'm sorry. You must be in pain."

"A little sore. The wounds are healing."

He grabbed my hand and directed me along the hallway to his bedroom. Once inside, he slowly peeled off my clothes and then picked me up. He carried me to his bathroom, setting me on the vanity, and turned on the steamy shower. He took off his clothes as the heat billowed around us.

I caught myself staring and cleared my throat. His body, from chest to wrists, was a wonderland of beautifully composed Japanese tattoos and other beast-themed ink. Stepping closer, he lifted my chin with a flick of his finger before leaning into my body and kissing me hard and deep. He sucked my tongue into his mouth. A fist in my hair angled my head back, granting him deeper access. My tongue slid around the tip of his and then rubbed under it. His growl vibrated through me, and I clenched my thighs.

He pulled his mouth away from me, and with a husky voice, he said, "Time to wash off the past and welcome our new beginning."

Pulling me into the stall with him, he sat on the shower seat, tugging me onto his lap, allowing the water to cascade onto both of us. Blood melted off his body, mingling with the water that went down the drain.

He moaned, as if enjoying the hot water beating against his sore muscles. I twisted around, facing him, my chest against his.

Kissing him hard on his lips, I crooned, "Let me take care of you, baby."

I made my way to my feet and put a dollop of body wash onto a washcloth before lathering it all over his body. Gently, I cleaned off all the wounds, sloughing away all the death and blood. It felt cathartic, as if we were starting anew. This would be a fresh beginning for us.

Dropping the washcloth to the floor, I grabbed the shampoo and lathered his hair, raking my fingernails against his scalp. He wrapped his arms around me, his mouth going to my nipple, taking turns and sucking each one into his greedy mouth.

"My turn," he uttered. He stood up and lathered up the washcloth. He paid special attention to my breasts and between my thighs. He lathered my hair, and as usual, the water transformed my flat-ironed hair into a cloud of tight ringlets. "I love your hair curly. It's sexy."

I smiled at him. "So you say, shifter."

He grabbed a strand of my hair. "It's wild, like you."

He turned off the water, pulled me out, and wrapped me in a towel. Now I was ready for anything, and before I knew it, he lifted me over his shoulder in a fireman carry.

I squealed, "Don't get cocky, wolfie."

"You haven't seen the meaning of cocky, baby." He brought me inside his bedroom and dropped me onto his bed.

Sitting up in the bed, I gave him a playful frown. "Okay, so now you think I'm going to let that thing"—I pointed to his huge thickness standing against his belly button—"anywhere near me?"

Jackal prowled toward me with narrowed eyes. "That's the plan, darling."

I raised my legs, knees spreading, with my folds glistening and ready for him. "And what makes you think your little plan is going to happen?"

Reaching the bed, he gently jerked my leg, sliding me to the edge of the mattress. "Because you're ready to accept the inevitable. You're mine, vampire, my mate, and tonight, you're going to keep quiet and take this cock like a big girl."

I bit my bottom lip. "So... I'm your mate, am I?"

"Darling, there's no other woman for me. And there's no other man for you. Now submit and let the fucking commence."

I smirked. "I'm all yours for the fucking... been for days, you damn cunt-tease." I pursed my lips. "But if you think I'm going to turn into one of those simpering women who bows to her mate after being claimed, then I'm not the woman for you."

"Only bowing I want is in our bedroom with you on your knees and my cock down your throat." He rumbled impatiently, "Why are we talking so much? I need to be so deep into your pussy that you can taste me in your throat."

I seriously studied him. "You know it won't be easy for Others to accept us as a couple, given the animosity between vampires and shifters."

"Nope, it won't." He nipped my bottom lip. "You're mine, vampire. Fuck anyone who doesn't like it."

"Damn, shifter... that's kind of hot."

He kissed my forehead, then my cheeks, and finally planted a kiss on my lips. "And just for the record, I'm not looking to change you. I love you the way you are."

I smiled impishly. "Wow, the shifter loves me, warts and all."

"Damn right."

"Good, because I've decided to keep your crazy ass."

"Really? Decided? You had no choice, woman."

I grabbed his face between my palms and kissed him hard. He seized the opportunity with hard lips, kissing me with such intensity that my pussy quivered with want.

He clutched my face with both hands, intimately pressing his forehead against mine.

Damn, his mere touch made me ready to bear his children.

He pulled back. "Now let's get the formalities out of the way. You belong to me, and I belong to you. I haven't touched or looked at another woman in weeks."

"Better not have."

"Now, get on all fours, darling. It's time for me to make your toes curl."

A tremor went through my body as my channel contracted. I ran my tongue over his firm lips, letting go of my fears and distrust caused by every man who had steered me wrong in my life. Jackal was the man for me.

"I want everything you're offering, shifter." I grabbed his hair. "There is no other man like you. I want us... forever." I paused. "And I'll love your crazy ass forever, too."

His eyes softened. "I love you, too, Reason."

✻ 15 ✻

JACKAL

THERE WERE SO many sides to Reason—sexy, rebellious, sassy, smart, and vulnerable—and I wanted them all.

Leaning in, she licked my lips and then plunged into my mouth with a persistent tongue. It slid around the tip of mine and then rubbed underneath. I thought about her doing that to my cock, and I almost exploded.

Dammit!

I couldn't hold back any longer, not with her soft and pliant in my arms.

Groaning, I plundered, possessed, and nipped at her full lips. I straddled her, one knee on each side of her waist. She stared up at me, her eyes dilated. Her sensuous mouth curved into a smile.

I leaned down, biting her bottom lip. "I can't get enough of you."

She trailed her fingers across my chest. "I'm yours, Jackal. Fuck me."

I simply growled in response. Wasting no time, I slid two fingers into her heat, stretching her open. She tightly squeezed those fingers, and I moaned just imagining how good she would feel around my staff.

"So beautiful," I murmured with approval as I slid down.

Molding her breasts with my hands, I sucked and bit each nipple until she was writhing beneath me, and then I journeyed down her body, pressing my mouth against her stomach, nibbling and kissing until all she seemed to want was to burst into flames.

"I'm getting ready to spread your legs wide open and lick your sweet slit, darling."

Rising up on my elbows, I hungrily surveyed her before pushing her legs out a little. Now she was even more exposed and vulnerable. I pressed her knees outward, tipping her pussy up in the air while looking straight into her eyes.

"This cunt is mine to do with as I please."

I slid my fingers between the wet folds of her heat. She arched up, wiggling closer, as my thumb circled and played with her clit.

"Whether it's with my cock or mouth, this pussy is all mine."

I stroked her smoldering wetness. She shivered as if she were on the verge of exploding. But I had no intention of letting her do that until she offered what I needed to hear—her soft request.

"Jackal," she whispered, "I... need—dammit. Please lick my pussy." Her breathing was ragged.

"My pleasure."

My hands curled around her thighs, spreading her wider. Hooking her legs over my shoulders, I settled myself between the V of her thighs.

"Who does this pussy belong to?" I gritted out while pinning her.

Showing her no damn mercy, my tongue flicked her swollen nub until she screamed, "Oh my fucking God!"

She bucked as I continued to bathe her with my mouth.

"Whose is it, Reason?" I thrust two fingers into her trembling channel, curving them inside her while pressing my thumb on her clit so my hand was clamped around her.

She wailed, "Yours," like a prayer.

I pulled my head back, watching how her skin glowed and

her eyes dilated as my fingers continued to stretch her. "Louder, Reason."

Her fingers gripped the sheets. "Dammit, Jackal."

"Louder," I demanded.

"It's yours."

With one seamless motion, I withdrew my fingers, gripped her ass, and stabbed my tongue inside her. Her back arched, and her legs moved to the back of my head as she cried out loudly. Consumed with lust, I continued relentlessly fucking her with my tongue.

Her fingers reached down, biting into my scalp, while I pumped her, drawing out her climax. Pulling her ass cheeks apart, I plunged one wet finger into the normally forbidden zone —her ass. She panted, drawing ragged breaths.

Mercifully, I relented, pulling away. Panting and wasted, she lay boneless with eyes blazing with a focused animal wildness. I lifted her chin with a flick of my finger and kissed her hard and deep. It was a kiss of utter possession.

I broke off the exchange and growled, "Turn around, face-down, and present your beautiful ass to me. Now."

She flipped onto her belly, and I guided her up onto her knees. She mewled when I bit her neck. I brushed my lips over her shoulders, and then, continuing on, I rained kisses along her spine.

Nudging her forward onto her hands, I massaged her buttocks. "You have the most gorgeous ass," I rumbled, running a hand across the curve of it before parting her cheeks. I touched her folds so intimately she gasped. "Fuck. You're so wet for me."

Reaching over to the nightstand, I pulled out a condom. I tore the package open with my teeth and quickly removed the latex. In seconds, I sheathed my cock and curled my hand in her hair, snapping her head back. "Your pussy. Your ass. All of you. Mine," I whispered into her ear.

Releasing her hair, I pressed her face down onto the bed and buried myself so far inside her that her whole body quaked from the sheer force. As wet as she was, it was still a snug fit.

"Oh, fuck!" she cried out as I ruthlessly stretched her.

My engorged flesh sank deeper between her sensitive folds, and my balls slapped against her wet heat. Her hips bucked.

With fingers buried into the flesh at her hips, I held her still. "Slow, darling. I don't want to hurt you." I gave her core time to adjust to my girth.

Her body tensed, as if adjusting to my fullness in her center.

"Relax, darling."

She took a deep breath.

Slowly, I eased out and back in, then I increased my speed from a sensuous slide to hard, forceful pumping. "Fuck!" I cursed.

She was driving me crazy with lust, and each stroke was bringing me closer and closer to the edge.

"Jackal," she groaned as I continued to fuck her like a man possessed.

She looked so comfortable against my skin.

"Don't stop," she whispered, shivering, as she gripped the bedsheets.

My fingers clutched the sides of her lush hips. I reared back and plunged in forcefully while nailing her clit with every stroke. Her core tightened around my cock. Her legs quivered. I drove deeper.

"You and me, together, until the wheels fall off, darling, for better or for worse," I stated roughly, thrusting faster.

"Yes. For better or for worse, Jackal." Her lovely keening echoed in the room.

"Fuck!" I cursed when she moved again.

"I'm going to come," she wailed.

"Not until I allow you."

Abandoning my control, I thrust short and fast and groaned in pleasure. She rocked back into me, taking everything I had to give. Our slick bodies were in perfect synchrony, a strange magnetic energy encircling us.

"Jackal, please."

Feeling everything inside me draw up, my body begged for sweet release. "Now!" With a low groan, I plunged in to the hilt before I felt the orgasm ripping up my spine, tearing through my limbs.

Reason's core spasmed around me hard while she shouted my name at the top of her lungs.

My fingers squeezed her hips. Again and again, I pulled out and plunged back inside her like a man on a mission and came so hard that I almost blacked out from the pure euphoric sensation. I slumped over her, catching my weight on my hands.

I nuzzled her neck. "All of you, mine."

Settling in the juncture of her neck and shoulder, I scraped my teeth over the spot, signaling what was to come. I bit down, breaking the skin. Reason moaned. I sucked strongly on the patch of skin I'd bitten, not wanting to leave to chance that anyone would consider the distinct mark anything but a claiming... by me.

It was done. I'd marked her body as my own. I would kill for her, live for her, do anything I needed to protect her.

We stayed glued to each other—me draped over her, my face buried in the crook of her neck.

Pulling back, I growled my approval, admiring my work, before swiping my tongue over the mark. I pressed my mouth to the top of her shoulder before pulling gently out of her.

"Let me take care of the condom." I disappeared for a second to dispose of it.

When I came back, tremors ran through her as my lips trailed across her shoulder. I pulled her farther up on the bed. I clutched her body against mine and kissed her neck, her chin, and her cheek before pushing the damp strands of hair away from her forehead.

"I love you, Reason." I leaned forward and softly kissed her.

She placed her hands on the sides of my face, stroking my jaw, as she stared deep into my eyes. "And I love you, shifter," she whispered.

Breathing in her sultry, rich scent, I brushed her nipple with the backs of my knuckles, and when she sighed, her lips curled up into a contented smile. I'd never seen anything more beautiful than Reason. Feeling the sweetness of the moment, I devoured her mouth with sweeping strokes of my tongue, slow and deep.

I couldn't believe how lucky I was to find her, a woman who was intelligent, independent, devastatingly compassionate and precious. Reason had discovered me, even in the depths of darkness when the sadness had left me broken and in despair.

She was all mine. My mate.

A gift that fate and the universe had bestowed.

She was truly my reason to love.

~

THANK YOU FOR READING **REASON TO LOVE!**

More Shifter Alpha goodness continues with **BEAUTY AND THE ALIEN BEAST!**

A fun, sexy, standalone action-packed sci-fi alien warrior romance featuring an irresistible alien warrior and the woman he wants forever.

GET A FREE SEDONA VENEZ BOOK!

https://sedonavenez.com/free-book

WANT FREE SEDONA VENEZ BOOKS?

Sign up for Sedona Venez's Newsletter and receive FREE BOOKS. In addition to the free stories, you will also get special pricing, exclusive previews and news of new releases.

GET A FREE SEDONA VENEZ BOOK!

Join Sedona's mailing list to be the first to know of new releases, free books, special prices and other author giveaways.

https://sedonavenez.com/free-book

OTHER TITLES BY SEDONA VENEZ

SciFi Romance
Galaxy Alien Warriors - The Box Set
Beauty and the Alien Beast

Paranormal Romance
Shifter Alphas Furever Series
Claimed by Her Two Alphas
Claimed by Her Wolf
Claimed by Her Bear
Claimed by Her Dragon

Paranormal Romance
Credence Curse Series
When Lightning Strikes
Taming the Beast
Reason to Love

Wolf Shifter Romance
Wolf Elite Series
Operation Wolf: Gunner
Operation Wolf: Eli

Operation Wolf: Hunter

Bears Shifter Romance
Bear Elite Series
Bear's Mission

Enemies-to-Lovers Romance
Dirty Secrets Series
Twisted Lies
Twisted Lies 2
Twisted Lies 3
Twisted Lies 4

Friends-to-Lovers Romance
Heart of Fire

MFM Ménage Romance
Standalone
Shameless Desires

Billionaire Boss Romance
Standalone
Mr. Billionaire CEO

Urban Fantasy Romance
Magic Fire Collection

ABOUT THE AUTHOR

USA TODAY BESTSELLING AUTHOR SEDONA VENEZ lives in New York City with her hot ex-military hubby—hooah—and their fur babies. She loves writing sizzling, sexy intricate stories about strong but broken characters who push limits, overcome their fears and risk it all for love.

Sedona loves to connect with readers!
www.sedonavenez.com